Unveiled

Vargas Cartel Series, Book 2

Lisa Cardiff

Unveiled

Limitless Publishing, LLC
Kailua, HI 96734
www.limitlesspublishing.com

Formatting: Limitless Publishing

ISBN-13: 978-1-68058-158-4
ISBN-10: 1-68058-158-9

Dedication

To my Dad. I miss you every day.

Chapter One

Hattie

"Hattie, baby." Evan's arms circled my waist. "You're safe."

"I'm safe," I answered weakly, my hands hooking like talons into the hem of my dress. The idea of reciprocating his embrace twisted my stomach into knots. I didn't feel safe. I felt alone, adrift. Ryker had severed every last rope tethering me to reality.

Evan's fingers tangled in my hair and he lifted my face, forcing me to look him in the eye. Guilt heated my cheeks like a scarlet letter. Shuttering my thoughts, I grudgingly held his soul-searching gaze. One of his hands trailed down the side of my face, along my jaw, and pausing over the mark Ryker left on my neck last night.

"What's this?"

A mixture of guilt, shame, and anger pumped through my veins. I bit the inside of my cheek and inhaled through my nose, pushing away the kaleidoscope of emotions. "I don't know. I've been drugged, tied to a chair, choked, cut by a knife, shot at, locked in a room, and that's just naming a few of the things that happened over the last few weeks. Do you plan to inventory all my injuries on the side of the highway, or can it wait?"

He withdrew his hands and backtracked a few steps. "You're right. I'm sorry. I'm just glad I have you back. The rest will sort itself out."

I rubbed the back of my neck. "Can you get my suitcase out of the trunk?"

"Sure." He grabbed my small, blue hard-shelled bag and transferred it to his car.

"What are we going to do with that car?"

"Leave it on the side of the road."

He opened the back door of the car, and I slipped into the seat, pressing my body as snugly as possible to the opposing door.

"Hattie, I missed you," he said after ten minutes of painful silence.

He draped his arm over my shoulder and his leg pressed against the length of mine. We'd sat like this at least a hundred times in the past as some faceless driver chauffeured us to and from an event for his father or some charity function. This time, however, our proximity felt stilted and uncomfortable. Evan felt it too. His body was stiff against mine, and lines bracketed his thinned lips.

"I'm sorry I snapped at you. What happened to me wasn't your fault."

He didn't abduct me. He didn't reject me. He didn't kick me out of his life and tell me to be with someone else. Ryker did. Yet somehow, I couldn't summon any hatred. He sent me away because he cared about me. It was the only ending possible, but the knowledge didn't stop my heart from dying a little with every growing mile between Ryker and me.

"You can lash out at me. I can take it. Whatever you need me to be, I'll do it."

He squeezed my hand. "If you need someone to be your punching bag, then I'm your man."

Sobs split through my lips, and hot tears burned like lava down my cheeks. My chest felt hollow. My head throbbed. I couldn't take this. Any of it. I didn't want Evan to be nice to me. He should hate me. I hated myself. He would hate me too if he found out what I did with Ryker.

"Shh," Evan whispered, pulling my head against his shoulder. "Don't cry. Remember what I said when you called me?"

"About wanting to be together again?"

"Yes." He stroked the back of my head. "I don't care what happened in the past, and by the past, I mean everything before we got in this car together."

I lifted my head from his shoulder. "But—"

He pressed two fingers to my lips, interrupting me. "I love you, Hattie, and I think you still love me. That's all I care about. The rest of it doesn't matter." He slipped his hand into his pocket and pulled out a black velvet box.

My stomach flipped. "No, Evan. I can't do this. Not right now." I blinked, barely able to see through the haze of tears.

"Just listen." Evan slid the ring on my finger, and I covered my face, refusing to look at him or the ring. "Here's what I'm proposing with this

3

ring." I shook my head. "Hattie, please open your eyes."

I sucked in a jagged breath and pried my eyes open. "Yes."

"I hurt you. You need more time to get over what I did and what happened over the last few weeks."

"I do." I wiped the tears from my face.

"That's fine, but in the meantime, I want you to wear this ring, and I want to announce our engagement."

"Why?"

He slanted forward and leaned his forehead against mine. "Because I want everyone to know I'm standing by you through this, and so is my family."

"I don't care what other people think," I protested halfheartedly.

"I do. I want people to see you as a survivor, not a victim."

"What does this ring have to do with that?"

He scraped his chapped lips across mine, and I jerked my head back. I couldn't be intimate with him. Not yet. Maybe never. This was so confusing.

"I need everyone, including you, to know I support you and love you no matter what."

"Evan, I don't want to rush into anything."

He threaded his fingers through mine and lifted my hand to his lips, kissing the inside of my wrist. "We're not rushing into anything. From the first moment I saw you, I knew I wanted to marry you. This ring symbolizes us taking control of our lives and doing what we should've done right after we graduated from college. We're reclaiming our future…together."

I wished it were that simple. I wanted it to be that simple. Evan offered me a way to push forward and recapture everything I'd lost. Ryker's words floated through my mind.

"You're going to meet Evan where Highway 307 intersects with the road leaving the villa. Then, you're going to forget about me, about what happened between us, and you're going to give Evan his second chance."

I glanced out the window, staring sightlessly at the miles and miles of white sand and turquoise water. Evan didn't push. He didn't argue his case more than he had, but he didn't need to. Ryker had done it for him.

"Okay." A dull pain clawed up the walls of my chest and nausea churned in my gut. I agreed to give Evan a second chance. So what if the second chance included a marriage proposal. I had already lost Ryker—the only man I'd ever craved more than my next breath. He had burrowed under my skin and infiltrated my mind and heart. Did it matter who I spent my life with if it couldn't be him?

A smile split Evan's face. The old me would've drunk in the perfect symmetry of his face and smiled in response. The new me was dead inside, and working my lips into something resembling a smile seemed like too much effort. Would I ever shed the emptiness clinging to me like a shroud?

"Is that a yes?"

My throat constricted until I could barely suck in a breath, but I forced out my answer. "Yes."

He leaned in to kiss me, and I turned my head to

the side instead. This moment marked the beginning of the rest of my life. Less than a week ago, I didn't know if I'd have a future. I should've been happy. Overjoyed. Why did everything still feel so bleak? Pointless?

Chapter Two

Hattie

Two weeks later...

My fingers tapping my thigh, I glared at the white stick taunting me from the marble countertop one foot in front of me.

One line?
Two lines?
One line?
Two lines?

My heart battered my ribcage from a combination of too much adrenaline and too much fear. *How long did this take again?* I scoured the instructions for the fifth time in as many minutes. Two more minutes, and then I'd know whether my stupidity in Mexico gave me the one thing I couldn't explain away with silence or more lies: a baby.

I watched the clock on my phone, waiting for the additional one hundred and twenty seconds that crawled like one hundred and twenty hours to expire. When the clock moved from 7:32 to 7:34 a.m., I closed my eyes, bracing for the result.

Whatever happened when I opened my eyes, I'd deal with it. I didn't have to make a decision right away. I had time. I had choices. I had resources. I blew out an exaggerated breath and pried my eyes open one at a time. With shaking hands, I lifted the white stick.

One line.

Thank God.

I wasn't pregnant.

I settled onto the white tiled floor, my back pressed into the door still clutching the stick. Mindless tears tracked down my face, and for the first time since I got home, I felt like I could breathe. Really breathe.

I shoved my fist into my mouth to stifle the sobs gaining momentum second by second. Always conflicted. Relief warred with utter misery. I would've died a thousand soul-plundering deaths if I saw two lines, but one line eliminated the last connection I had with *him.* I couldn't say his name. Ever. I couldn't even think it. I'd tailspin into a chasm of melancholy before the second syllable of his name exited my mouth.

I was so fucked up. I wanted him. I hated him. Even nameless and unspoken, he infiltrated my body like a parasite, weaving his way into my brain. I couldn't stop thinking about him.

The way he smelled.

The way his velvety voice sent tremors down my spine.

The way it felt as he slid inside of me.

Pain cleaved through my chest as I strangled in the prison of my self-pity. This was harder than I'd thought. If I'd known returning to my real life was going to be so hard, I would've refused to leave the Vargas Cartel compound.

Bang.

Bang.

"Hattie," Evan hollered as he knocked on the bathroom door.

Go away.

Go away.

I held my breath, not making a sound, not moving an inch.

Leave me alone.

Bang.

"Hattie?" He yelled my name like a curse. Maybe I was cursed. I felt doomed. Doomed to a life of tragedy.

I rubbed my eyes with the palms of my hands. "Yes."

"Are you okay?"

I wished everyone would stop asking me that question. They wanted me to say yes. They expected me to say yes, but part of me wanted to tell the truth. I'd never be okay. I stopped being okay the minute I walked into that bar in Mexico…maybe before that.

"I'm fine," I answered instead. Nobody wanted the truth. The truth was ugly. I was lost. The Hattie I knew a couple of months ago had disappeared. No matter how many times I tried to pull my life together, I couldn't. Too many pieces of the puzzle were missing.

His feet shifted on the hardwood floors outside the door and the floor creaked.

"I made breakfast." I didn't respond. "Yogurt with chia seeds and fruit."

"Oh. Okay. Thanks," I said, wiping my nose with a tissue. I couldn't believe he knew what I liked for breakfast. We had lived together for two years, and he hadn't acknowledged my preference once.

The door handle rattled. "Will you unlock the door? You're scaring me."

My gaze dropped to the stick in my hand. *Shit*. I surged to my feet and tossed the stick along with the folded directions back into the box. I rolled it inside a towel and hid it in the cabinet under the sink.

If Evan found it, I would have a lot of explaining to do. I hadn't let him so much as kiss me on the lips since I moved back into his apartment the day after we flew back from Mexico. He slept on the pull out sofa bed every night, and I slept in the bedroom. He'd know the pregnancy test didn't have anything to do with him.

"Sorry," I mumbled as I cracked the door a few inches. Evan was fully dressed, his sandy brown hair perfectly gelled, and his jaw shaved with military precision.

The faint smile on his face evaporated. "Have you been crying?"

I glanced at the floor and rubbed my temples with my fingertips. My head throbbed from a combination of sleepless nights and nonstop bickering with Evan. "No. Not really."

"Hattie," Evan cautioned, closing his hands

around my upper arms. I jerked away before I could stop my reaction. I didn't want his hands on me. I never wanted his hands on me.

"I'm fine. Okay. Stop looking at me like I'm going to break."

He raked his hands through his hair, and his eyebrows knitted in confusion. Then, he shook his head, and his face hardened into a cold mask. "Jesus, Hattie. This is getting old. You flinch if I touch you. You still won't let me sleep in the bed with you. You turn to the side when I try to kiss you. You treat me like a stranger. What the hell? How long are we going to play this game?"

I slipped by him and walked to the kitchen. "What game?" I asked without glancing over my shoulder.

"You won't tell me anything about what happened, which is fine. I get it. You're still not ready to trust me, but you haven't told your therapist anything either."

I spun on my heel, my hair whipping the side of my face. Fear and anger skittered down my spine. "How the hell would you know what I tell my therapist?"

He held out his hands in front of him in mock surrender. "I don't. She hasn't told me anything except that you haven't opened up to her. That you've spent every session feeding her a bunch of uninformative answers."

"There's nothing to tell." My hands shaking, I lifted the coffee carafe and poured the dark liquid into a mug. "You know what happened. I was abducted, and now I'm home. That's it. Sitting in a room, dissecting every detail with a stranger won't miraculously heal me."

He slapped his hand against the countertop, rattling my coffee mug. "Dammit, Hattie. If you didn't have anything to tell, you wouldn't be acting like this."

I focused on the television streaming the morning news across the room. I couldn't look at him. I couldn't take this anymore. Every morning and every night we had the same conversation. It was an endless loop, replaying over and over. "It's only been two weeks. Can't you give me time to process everything that's happened? When I'm ready, I'll talk. I promise." I pinched the bridge of my nose and then whispered, "I'm trying. I really am. Don't give up yet."

He leaned his hips against the kitchen counter and sighed. "Okay. You're right. I won't push you. I promised we'd work through this together and we will."

I lifted my cup of coffee to my lips, letting the steam curl around my face. "I'm sorry. I wish I could offer you more." The last two weeks had passed in a blur of nothingness. Holed up in our small two-bedroom townhome, I went through the motions of living, but I felt detached from everything and everyone. Nothing seemed real anymore. I floated through life like a zombie...lifeless, brainless, and indifferent.

"I asked for a second chance. You moved back in. You're wearing the ring." He knitted his fingers through mine, lifting my hand, displaying the engagement ring he gave me two weeks ago. "But you can't be mad at me for wanting more."

"More?" My mind raced with the implications of his request. Could I give him more? I wanted to move on with my life, but was Evan the answer? I didn't know. The thought of being intimate with him repulsed me.

He swiveled around and pinned me against the countertop. "Yes. I want my girlfriend back. I want the woman I've loved for the last four years back. I want to hold you. I want to kiss you. I want to laugh with you. I want to make you happy again. Is that so bad?"

I swallowed over the lump lodged in my throat. "I wish I could be her again, but I'm not sure it's possible."

"Anything's possible." He rubbed his hands up and down my arms. "But you have to get up every day and try."

He was right. I barely left the house anymore. I went to the therapist twice a week. I ate dinner at my parents' house every Sunday. That's it. I took a leave of absence from school, and instead of graduating next month, I'd put it off indefinitely. Vera had been blowing up my phone every day since I stepped foot off the plane with Evan. I never answered her calls, but I did send her a text every day or two. I couldn't face her yet. She'd want answers. Answers I wasn't ready to give. Answers I might never be ready to give.

"Maybe."

He leaned forward, his lips only inches from mine. My mind pleaded with me to push him away. Instead, I squeezed my eyes shut and forced my muscles to melt into him. I needed to let go of the past and move forward. That meant exploring if there was anything left between Evan and me. His lips brushed across mine. I balled my hands into fists.

I can do this.

I can do this.

I tilted my head to the side and parted my lips, pushing my limits, moving outside of my comfort zone. He tasted like coffee and toothpaste all mixed together. His tongue moved against mine, testing my willingness.

It's not bad.

I'm not hurting anyone.

I'm not cheating.

Slowly, I uncurled my fists, breathing through my nose. My eyes popped open, and I studied his face. His eyes were closed. He looked relaxed...peaceful even. I counted to ten in my head. *Eight, nine, ten*...and that was all I could manage for today.

I turned my head to the side, breaking the kiss. "Stop."

He backpedaled a few micro-steps and nodded. I wiped the back of my hand across my mouth, and he flinched as though I hit him.

"I'm sorry," I said for at least the hundredth time in the last week. "I just..." My voice faded to silence, and I shook my head from side to side almost imperceptibly. "I don't know." How could I explain why I stopped kissing him? Why didn't I want to kiss him? Sleep with him? I couldn't, unless I revealed the whole sordid story of my abduction and how I still wanted *him*, the man who abducted me.

"No, it's okay." He smiled, his eyes dancing with mischief, and if I weren't completely miserable and disgusted with myself, I would've savored his happiness and committed it to memory. "It's progress."

My shoulders sagged in defeat, and I repressed a long sigh. "Yeah, I guess. What are you doing today?"

"I have a few things to take care of at school, and then my mom and I are going to lunch."

"Really?" Evan rarely spent one on one time with his mom.

"Yep. We have a party to put together, and you know how my mom loves to plan."

"What kind of party?" I asked, my heart stuttering in my chest.

"It was supposed to be a surprise. My mom wanted it to be a surprise, but I don't want you to panic."

My eyes flared, and my stomach somersaulted. "A surprise?"

"My parents are hosting an engagement party for us next weekend."

My mouth opened and then closed in rapid succession. The edge of my vision blurred. My knees wobbled, and I braced my elbows on the countertop so I didn't collapse. My emotions seesawed up and down, but mostly down. Always and inevitably down.

"Breathe, Hattie, breathe."

His words ricocheted through my soul like

slivers of glass. "I can't do it. I'm not ready," I finally blurted out.

"It's time, Hattie. Even your therapist agreed it'd be okay to take this step forward. You have ten days to prepare yourself to join the world of the living again. You'll be fine."

Panicked, I shook my head from side to side. "No," I whispered, but it came out more like a groan than a word.

Evan moved forward, closing the space between our bodies. He grabbed my hands, but instead of feeling comforted, I felt like I was suffocating under the weight of his expectations.

"Hattie. I won't leave your side the entire night. If you're uncomfortable, squeeze my hand and we'll leave. We can do this."

"I don't want anyone to ask me about Mexico. I can't talk about it."

"That's fine. I'll have my mom put out the word."

A nervous laugh tumbled out of my mouth. "Evan, please, your mom can't control every conversation."

"Then you don't know my mom as well as you think you do."

I fell silent for a few excruciating seconds as I evaluated my options. I didn't have any options. I was out of time. I couldn't hide forever. "Okay. I'll do it."

Evan yanked my body against his, gathering me into a tight embrace. "Thank God," he murmured next to my ear. "You'll see. This party is going to be good for us. It's the first step to taking our life back."

I hoped like hell he was right because I couldn't stand my life anymore. Something had to change.

Chapter Three

Ryker

"What in the hell are you doing here, Rever?"

I tossed my keys on the table in my entryway, and they slid across the empty surface, hitting the wall. My home wasn't much of a home, more like a pit stop between jobs. After five years, I still hadn't hung a single picture or bought one rug to cover the hardwood floors. In truth, I thought it was a waste of money and time. I hadn't found a true home since I graduated from high school. I'd been too busy making a name for myself.

Rever shrugged and crossed one ankle over his thigh. He looked like a younger version of our dad, Ignacio Vargas. Dark hair. Dark eyes. A long, angular nose. Same height. Same build. If I didn't know better, I'd think I had traveled back in time. He even moved his body the same way.

"I was out of options."

"What made you believe showing up at my house was an option?" We'd never been on friendly terms. We'd come to blows more than once in our life. We were nearly the same age, but we had different mothers, and that made all the difference in the world. Rever was legitimate whereas I was a bastard. His legitimacy entitled him to everything the Vargas Cartel had to offer. My illegitimacy entitled me to nothing. I didn't even use the Vargas name except when I traveled to Mexico. In the United States, I was Ry Fallon. Fallon was my mom's maiden name and the name on my birth certificate.

"The process of elimination." He stood up and crossed the room. "I couldn't stay in Mexico, and you're the only other family I have."

"Why can't you stay in Mexico?"

"Don't play dumb."

I folded my arms across my chest. I hadn't seen Rever in over three years, and I couldn't claim I'd missed him. "I'm sure Ignacio will forgive you. He always does. This time won't be any different." My words were unintentionally bitter. I didn't envy Rever. I never truly wanted what he had. The burden of leading the Vargas Cartel wasn't something I'd wish on my worst enemy, and even with our never-ending feud, Rever didn't qualify as an enemy. He was something in between.

Rever had caused more than his fair share of trouble in the last ten years. Rather than following in Ignacio's footsteps, he barely showed a passing interest in becoming the successor to the Vargas Cartel. He overindulged in everything.

Drugs.

Women.

Gambling.

His arrogance landed him in a U.S. prison three months ago for money laundering, and I had to negotiate his release.

"I'm done with the Vargas Cartel. I don't want to play by Ignacio's rules anymore."

I snorted. "You never played by his rules. That's how you ended up in jail."

Rever fisted his hands, and he smiled coldly. "You want to be the heir apparent for the Vargas Cartel? Well, you can have it. I don't have any interest in killing people for perceived slights and smuggling drugs—"

"Exactly. You're just interested in using the drugs and spending the money. You don't want any of the responsibilities that go along with it."

He snatched his black leather jacket off the back of a chair. "You're right."

I rocked back on my heels and narrowed my eyes. "Right about what?"

"I shouldn't have come here." His gaze drifted to the floor. "For some reason, I got it in my head that you'd help me, but apparently, I was wrong. You don't consider me family. You never have." Rever stuffed his arms into the sleeves of his jacket.

"That's not true," I growled. "I negotiated your release. I didn't have to do it, but I did. I got you out of that prison. I could've walked away and told Ignacio to find someone else to help you."

"You should've left me there. Ignacio is going to kill me."

"No, he won't," I said with absolute certainty. Ignacio had done a lot of horrible things in his life, but he'd never purposely hurt his children. As much as he loved the cartel, he loved his children more—especially Rever. Sure, he'd make Rever pay for what he did, but he wouldn't kill him.

Rever shoved his hands into his pockets. "Once he knows everything, he will kill me," he said quietly.

I didn't say anything for a drawn out second as I ran my hand down the side of my face. "Everything? What do you mean by everything?" I finally asked, pushing my apprehension aside. My sources confirmed Rever's account of the events from the time he was arrested until he was released. According to them, he hadn't revealed Senator Deveron's connection to the Vargas Cartel, but what did I know? Sources lied all the time.

"Anna Alvarez is pregnant."

"Am I supposed to know who that is?"

"Juan Alvarez's daughter."

My brows furrowed. "Juan Alvarez…as in the head of the Alvarez Cartel?"

He paled momentarily and then squared his shoulders. "Yes."

Swallowing the dread inching up the walls of my chest, I shifted on my feet. "I'm going to ask the question, even though I think I already know the answer. Are you the father?"

"Yes."

My blood ran cold. "Fuck, Rever. We've barely tolerated each other our entire life. Why would you come to me? Why do you think I can save you? I don't have any influence over Ignacio, much less Juan Alvarez. My hands are tied."

I didn't want to deal with this. When I drove out

of the Vargas Cartel compound over three weeks ago, I never intended to go back. I planned to sever every last string tethering me to that place. That world. That life. Negotiating Rever's release from prison was supposed to be my last job for them.

"I need you to help me get Anna out of there."

"What? How?"

"I don't know. You abducted the attorney general's daughter. Find a way to abduct Anna and bring her to me. I'll figure out the rest."

A laugh nearly escaped my mouth, but I bit my lip, stifling the urge. Rever was deadly serious. He actually expected me to fly back to Mexico, abduct a drug lord's daughter, and smuggle her where? To the United States. It was fucking crazy. Bat shit crazy.

"Do you have any idea what is going on between the Vargas and the Alvarez Cartels right now? They are tearing each other apart as we speak. Dead bodies are piling up. The feud has even made its way into the U.S. newspapers a few times."

"I understand what that means better than you do." He rubbed the back of his neck as he paced back and forth. "I've lived that life for almost thirty years. Do you know how much blood is on my hands?" His voiced cracked on the last word.

I shook my head. "Ignacio protected you from that side of the cartel. He never made you kill anyone."

A shadow crossed his face, and he paled. "Not with my hands, but I did it with my words too many times to count. Why do you think I ran? It was for her. For our child. I refuse to continue the cycle."

He shook his head slowly back and forth. "The Vargas Cartel will not claim my child."

"Why now? Since when do you give a shit about anyone but yourself?" I'd heard the stories. Rever had a gambling addiction and a recreational drug problem. So many women had drifted through his life over the last ten to twelve years, he probably didn't remember a third of them.

He tugged on the collar of his shirt. "Since I met her. She changed everything. She changed me."

My eyes flickered to the window behind him. A couple of months ago, I would've laughed at his words, but not anymore. Not after Hattie. Hattie had infected my mind and poisoned me with her smile and golden eyes. She changed me, but I hadn't decided if it was a good thing. In my line of work, attachments complicated everything.

"Fine. I'll help you," I murmured as I plopped down into a chair in my living room. Even as I said it, I knew I'd regret getting involved in Rever's life. Nothing good would come out of this, and if I abducted Anna Alvarez, everyone would know. The border between the U.S. and Mexico wouldn't mean a damn thing if the Alvarez Cartel traced her disappearance back to me. I'd be as good as dead.

"How fast can you do it?"

"A month, maybe two."

"No," Rever yelled. "It has to happen within the next week or two."

"Things like this take planning. I can't just snatch her from Alvarez territory and put her on a plane. I need to know her habits, her friends' habits, her family's habits."

Rever slammed his hand on the back the chair. "I can give you all the information you need."

"I need a viable plan or she won't make it out alive."

"I have to get her away from her family and out of Mexico before she starts showing."

"How long is that?"

"Fuck. I don't know. One to three weeks. Not long."

I glanced at my wristwatch, then shook my head. I didn't have time for this tonight. "I don't know if I can pull it off. Are you planning to stay here tonight?"

"I can't go anywhere else. In case you forgot, I'm not exactly a welcome visitor in the U.S. I need to keep a low profile."

I cocked my head to the side. "How did you get across the border, anyway?"

"The border is more porous than it has been in years, but to answer your question, I used a drug smuggling tunnel from Sonora, Mexico to Naco, Arizona. Once I made it to Arizona, I borrowed an associate's car."

My eyes narrowed. "Borrowed or stole?"

Rever lifted one shoulder and dropped it. "The details aren't important."

"Out of curiosity, how much does it cost to smuggle someone across the border these days?"

He smirked. "We charge thirty-five hundred to smuggle a person on foot, and eight grand using loaded eighteen-wheelers. It's easy money. The Vargas Cartel made about six million dollars smuggling people over the border last year, and it

24

diverts law enforcement's attention away from our drug smuggling activities."

"How's that?" I asked, even though I didn't want to know. The depravity of the drug smuggling business stopped surprising me years ago.

"You leave a group of people on the river bank or an open area where border patrol can easily find them. They draw all the attention while the drug smugglers slip over the border undetected."

I stood up and headed for my bedroom. "I have to get ready."

"Where are you going?"

"I have plans," I answered without glancing over my shoulder, suddenly feeling older than I had in years. Once again, I was being sucked into a life I wanted to leave far behind. I should've shoved Rever out the door or called the authorities and had him arrested, but I wouldn't do it. Ignacio had drummed the need for family loyalty into my head for as long as I could remember. As much as I wished I could abandon them, I wouldn't.

"Don't you think you should cancel and spend the night strategizing with me?"

"No. I have an engagement party to attend."

"An engagement party? For who?"

"Hattie Covington."

Rever's dark eyes narrowed into glittering slits, and his mouth pressed into a firm line. "You're playing with fire. This game is going to blow up in your face."

"Don't you think I know that?"

He groaned under his breath. "Then why are you going?"

"Because I want to see her."

"That's a dumb reason."

"You asked a dumb question."

Chapter Four

Hattie

"Hattie," my mom said the minute Evan and I walked into Senator Deveron's home for our engagement party.

She air-kissed my cheek, a frozen smile on her face. She looked as perfect and as icy as I remembered. Every strand of her blonde hair was immaculately groomed into an elegant twist, highlighting her sharp cheekbones and the curve of her jaw. She wore an ivory tailored suit with subtle fringed trim, buttoned flap pockets, large jeweled buttons, and princess seams. She looked like the perfect politician's wife. She *was* the perfect politician's wife. Unfortunately, she was far from the perfect mother, or at least my idea of the perfect mother.

Some small portion of me had believed my mom would behave like a normal parent after I returned from Mexico. Less than fifteen minutes into our first conversation, I realized nothing had changed. She truly subscribed to the notion that you shouldn't let a crisis go to waste. She scolded me for going to Mexico, for breaking up with Evan, and for being abducted.

"Mom. It's nice to see you," I said, taking a few anemic steps away from her.

As my eyes drifted over the smiling faces of our family, friends, and business associates, I felt nothing. Not happiness. Not sadness. Just a complete lack of interest in everyone and everything around me.

"Where's Dad?"

"He and Senator Deveron had a few things to discuss before the party gets into full swing. He should join us any minute."

I nodded absently as Evan slid his arm around my hips. As irrational as it sounded, I wished he'd stop touching me. Instead of saying anything, I leaned into him, pretending for the moment he meant something to me and I still loved him.

I scanned the white flower arrangements advantageously placed all over the Deverons' home. I hated white. If my mom or Evan's mom had consulted me, I would've never picked white anything. After spending too many days staring at the white walls and floors at the Vargas Cartel compound, I hated the absence of color.

If I had my choice, I would've selected red roses. Red seemed more appropriate given the circumstances of our engagement. Red was the color of blood, the color of anger, the color of sacrifice—and tonight marked the moment when I'd sacrifice everything.

The future I wanted.

My heart.
My soul.
My dreams.
My dignity.

All of it would evaporate into a pile of used up pixy dust the minute Evan announced our engagement, and I couldn't even be mad at Evan. He wasn't the one keeping secrets and living a lie. I fell in love with another man, but he didn't want me enough to fight for me, for us. I may have looked fine on the outside, but on the inside I was bleeding and broken.

Smiling, Evan handed me a glass of champagne from a small round table draped in white fabric. "Here they come now. My dad's going to give a toast."

Senator Deveron lifted his glass into the air, and the low murmurs stopped as all eyes focused on him. His trademarked veneered grin slid into place, and he cleared his throat. "When Evan first brought Hattie to our house, my wife and I fell in love with her. She's smart, beautiful, and kind. We knew she was the right woman for our son. So when Evan told us that Hattie agreed to marry him, we were thrilled. Evan, we are so proud of the adult you have become. With the love of your life at your side, nothing will be impossible. To Evan and Hattie."

Clapping, cheering, and congratulations floated through the air, and I felt disconnected from the moment. It didn't seem real. Nobody acknowledged my abduction. Nobody cared about my mental withdrawal. My life kept moving day after day.

My engagement party was planned.

Evan selected my ring.

Invitations were sent.

A therapist was hired.

My parents moved all my belongings into Evan's house.

Even my dress—an ivory silk crepe dress with a blouson silhouette—was ordered and delivered to Evan's townhome by my mom. It didn't look like something I'd pick, but then again, neither was my life. Not anymore. I'd lost control of everything.

"It's bad luck not to take a drink," Evan whispered next to my ear.

Not making eye contact with him, I lifted the glass to my lips as my eyes scanned the room, but I didn't take a sip. I didn't know why. It was childish, but I considered it my final symbolic rebellion before I entered a loveless marriage. One I didn't want. One I wouldn't want no matter how many days passed.

Suddenly, time froze. My muscles tensed the minute I saw *him*, Ryker Vargas. Just whispering his name inside the relative safety of my mind caused my heart to knock savagely against my breastbone. For a fraction of a second, I thought I was hallucinating, that my brain was playing vindictive tricks on me. My vision tunneled until all I could see was him, standing across the room—a wicked smile dancing at the corners of his lips, an island all to himself, sucking the energy out of the room. Our eyes locked and nobody existed except the two of us.

I swayed on my feet, and I realized I hadn't taken a breath in over thirty seconds. The shock of seeing him had sucked every last molecule of air from my lungs. Numb, the champagne glass slipped from my hand, and the bubbly liquid splashed on my legs and the top of my nude-colored heels.

"Are you okay?" Evan whispered next to my ear as he wrapped his arm around my shoulder. His mouth swept across the corner of my lips and my stomach churned with acid.

I tugged at the suddenly too tight collar of my dress. "I don't feel good. I need to sit down for a minute," I said absently, my eyes anchored to Ryker's in a silent battle. He looked exactly as I remembered, only better.

A black suit hugged his muscular body, barely containing his broad shoulders. Rough stubble shadowed the rugged angles of his golden skin, and my fingers itched to trace the strong line of his jaw. His gray eyes were hooded, a knowing smirk on his face. With his legs crossed at his ankles, he relaxed against the wall in a way most people would mistake for languid elegance. I knew better. He was a predator ready to attack. Conquer. Take what he wanted.

With his hand on my lower back, Evan guided me out of the room. I followed his cues for a few steps, then I froze mid-stride. "No. You stay here and talk with everyone. Both of us can't leave the party. I'll slip to your dad's study and sit down for a few minutes."

"No. I'm not leaving you." He squeezed my arm. His fingers were like daggers digging into my skin. On some level, he probably thought I'd disappear if he didn't keep me close. Maybe I would.

I twisted out of his grasp, and my legs moved rapidly, eating up the distance between the study and me. I didn't know if I was running to or from Ryker, but I needed space. "I'll be back in twenty minutes. Maybe less. Nobody will notice."

"Hattie, I don't think that's a good idea."

My stomach somersaulted. He was right. Being alone wasn't a good idea, but neither was having a full-blown panic attack in the middle of our engagement party. I painted an overly bright smile on my face, and the corners of my lips protested their disuse. I couldn't remember the last time I had smiled. Really smiled from joy or anything that made me happy.

I pushed open one of the heavy double doors to his dad's study. The hinge creaked. "I'll be fine. If I'm not back in twenty minutes, you can come and get me." I waved my hand in the direction of the camel-colored loveseat near the bay window. "I'll be right there."

He scrubbed his hand down the side of his face, and then kissed my forehead. "Okay."

He turned around, and I watched until he disappeared around the corner. Then, I closed the door. When I heard the slow click of the door latch, my body sagged. Too many conflicting thoughts stumbled through my mind.

Why was Ryker here?

Did anyone know who he was?

Did he come back for me? My heart rate spiked at the thought.

Less than five minutes later, the door cracked open.

"Evan, it hasn't been twenty minutes," I said without turning around.

"Hattie?"

My lungs contracted, and I rotated on my heel.

"Ryker," I said, my voice barely a whisper as I backpedaled. "What are you doing here?"

His gray eyes glittered in the dim light as he stalked to me. Blood thundered through my veins, echoing in my ears. Every inch of my skin tingled with awareness. My nipples pebbled in anticipation of his touch.

Oh shit. This was not good. I shook my head from side to side. My lips wobbled. I couldn't let him touch me. If he did, I'd crumble like Humpty Dumpty. My razor-thin hold on sanity would vanish, and nothing could put me back together again.

"I wanted to see you." His velvet voice rolled over me like a caress.

"No." I folded my arms across my body like a shield, burrowing my fingernails into the flesh of my arms, striving to ground myself in reality. "You have to go. We agreed. You shouldn't be here."

"We didn't agree on anything." With a faint smile on his face, he reached out his hand casually. Too casually. My heart pleaded with me to grab his hand, launch myself at him, and never let go. But I didn't. Nothing good would come of this. We couldn't be together.

Like a broken record stuck on repeat, I continued shaking my head back and forth. "You told me to give Evan a second chance. That's what I'm doing. If you haven't noticed, that's what tonight is about.

This is my engagement party." My voice trembled on the last word, showing a chink in my armor.

He planted his hands on the wall beside my head, imprisoning me. "I noticed, but I changed my mind about us…about being with you."

His body slanted against mine until his lips were inches from my ear. I closed my eyes as his warm breath billowed along my neck, ruffling my hair. A shiver shot down my spine and goosebumps erupted on my arms. *This was bad. Really bad.*

Confused and on the verge of crying, I inhaled, desperately trying to track down every last ounce of my wilting willpower, but I regretted it instantly. His spicy, sea-salt scent filled my lungs, intoxicating me, weakening my defenses. I wanted him.

I opened my eyes, and he was close. Too close. I could see every individual eyelash and the charcoal rim around his irises. "You think it's that easy? That you can just declare you changed your mind, and I'll run back into your open arms?"

His eyes raked over my body like a predator inspecting his prey. "I know it is. I can see it on your face. You still want me." His lips playfully ran along the side of my neck, sucking on my pulse point, and I moaned. My brain took a leave of absence and my body went on autopilot. I unfolded my arms and looped them around his waist.

I condemned the familiarity of his touch and the sensation of his body against mine to hell. Every slide of his lips against my neck was a pleasurable form of torture. I shouldn't crave something so toxic to my sanity, but couldn't resist him. I never could. Time hadn't changed my reaction to him; it only made him more potent.

The air around us crackled and buzzed with unrestrained lust. My body felt like it would go up in flames any second, even as my ego still wept from his dismissal almost four weeks ago. I was standing on the edge of the cliff waiting for him to tell me to jump.

His hands bit into my hips, drawing me against him. Hip to hip. Chest to chest. Our lips only inches apart, my breathing quickened as I waited for him to make the next move. If he kissed me, claimed me, all bets were off. Everything would change. I didn't think I could give him up again. I'd fight for him.

"I missed you," I whispered more to myself than him.

Then, his lips crashed against mine, and I jumped into the rabbit hole of my destruction, surrendering to my inexhaustible weakness for him. I moaned as his tongue slipped through my parted lips. His hands tunneled into my hair, tilting my head back, demanding more, and I willingly gave him everything.

His forbidden, familiar taste made me lightheaded. I wished—not for the first time—that I could take a vaccine and make myself immune to him.

To his charm.

To his smile.

To his smell.

Fuck…I missed his smell. Nobody smelled like him. It was even headier than I remembered. My senses whirled every time I inhaled. I felt as if I had tumbled head first into his bed.

He groaned, and the sound ignited a frenzy inside of both of us. Static hummed in my ears. I didn't care that we were in my fiancé's childhood home celebrating my engagement to another man. We could've been in a room full of people for all I cared. My driving need for him made me delirious and impulsive. I buried my betrayal of Evan and our engagement deep in the convoluted chambers of my mind.

I needed him. I needed this more than anything else. It had been too long. We staggered even closer to each other, and he braced his hand on the wall behind me to stop us from falling. I wanted to climb inside him and lay claim to his heart and soul, melding us together like two atoms in a nuclear fusion.

Chapter Five

Ryker

Everything I led myself to believe over the last few weeks disintegrated into dust the moment I came face to face with Hattie Covington again. How could I keep my bearings around her when my feelings for her crippled my judgment?

I planned to slip into the party and leave before she saw me. But the minute my eyes landed on her standing in front of the room, smiling prettily at Evan, their hands intertwined the slow burn of something resembling jealousy churned in my gut. At that instant, I knew I couldn't walk away without talking to her, touching her, kissing her, claiming her. I wanted to beat my chest and scream she was mine, not Evan's. That she'd never belong to him the way she belonged to me.

I wasn't accustomed to these messy emotions. The turmoil of a human psyche didn't have a place in my life. In the short time I'd known her, Hattie had succeeded in messing with my head until right and wrong had flipped on its axis. She made me feel something I had no right to feel.

"Hattie," I groaned when her hands slipped beneath my suit jacket, roaming impatiently over the starched fabric of my shirt. Fucking hell. We didn't have enough time to do everything I needed to do. The memory of the feel of her beneath me haunted me since I released her. I wanted to sling her over my shoulder and carry her out the front door. I had to be inside of her again. I needed to kiss, taste, and stroke every inch of her skin. The engagement party and the deal I made with Senator Deveron be damned.

For some reason, I got it in my head that if I put enough time and distance between us, my need for her would disappear. It didn't work. Far from it. Now that I held her in my arms again, I didn't want to let her go.

My hand traced the outline of her body until I reached the hem of her dress. Slowly, inch-by-inch, I slid the ivory, silky dress up her long legs. What I wouldn't give to have her legs wrapped around me again.

"Wait." She jerked back, dropping her hands to her sides. "This is crazy."

"I know. We should stop." Even as the words tumbled from my mouth, I slid my hand inside her panties barely an inch. There was something about claiming her right here and thumbing my nose in Senator Deveron's face that made me want to ignore common sense. Ignore reality. Ignore consequences.

She clamped her hand around my wrist. "No. I can't do this. Not here. Evan will come back any second. You need to leave. I don't know how I would explain this...you." Her voice trailed off and her face paled, as if the reality of the moment just clicked into place.

I snatched my hand away from her and inhaled a shuddering breath. My chest heaving, I spun around and shoved my hands into my pockets. She was right. This wasn't the time or the place for this, but I hated Evan believing he had a claim on her. I facilitated that claim, but it didn't make things any easier to stomach.

"Are you okay?" Hattie rested her head against my back. "Are you mad?" Her small fingers toyed with the back of my hair.

One simple touch and pleasure whistled down my spine. I wanted to be near her. I wanted her to care about me. I wanted her to love me even though I participated in the destruction of her life. I temporarily stole her freedom. I couldn't delude myself. Hattie should hate me. I abducted her. I tricked her. I was still lying to her. She could never know the real reason she was selected as a pawn in the deadly game between Senator Deveron and the Vargas Cartel.

As much as I wanted to believe otherwise, nothing had changed. Hattie and I could never be together. We were a house of cards. One soft breeze and we'd fall apart.

"I'm fine," I said, purposely not answering the second question because I was mad, but not at her. I was mad at myself for coming here, for participating in her abduction, for sending her home to Evan.

"Do you love him?" I asked, even though I had no right to an answer.

She sighed. "I don't know how to answer that. It's complicated."

I turned to face her and held my hand over her heart. "I want the real truth, not the truth you think I want to hear."

"I don't—"

Evan opened the door, pausing at the threshold. "Hattie?"

I brushed my knuckles against hers, back and forth. Evan's eyes locked on the transitory contact, and Hattie wrapped her arms around her torso, snatching her hand out of my reach.

"Do you know Ry Fallon?" Evan asked, his brows scrunched together. Most likely, he couldn't make sense of the current situation.

As far as he and Senator Deveron knew, I was an acquaintance who had expressed interest in bundling campaign funds for the Senator. A bundler pooled contributions from several donors with the same goals to fund a campaign. This loophole in the campaign finance reform laws gave corporations and lobbyists the ability to buy political influence.

Offering to bundle funds for the Senator was the perfect way to infiltrate his inner circle as Ry Fallon while doing my less than honest work as Ryker Vargas. My separate identities remained intact.

"Ry Fallon?" Hattie uttered. Her eyes flickered to mine briefly, then returned to Evan. "No. Not really. We just met actually." Her voice wavered. Did Evan know she had lied?

Evan rubbed his hand along his jaw line. "Ry's

done some work for my dad."

Hattie paled. "What kind of work?"

"We've talked about fundraising, but I haven't agreed to do anything," I clarified. I didn't want anyone to unravel the full extent of my duplicity. I led a double life—part of it in the light, and the other part in the shadows.

"You're right. Now that you mention it, my dad said nothing was final." He smiled, and then he focused his attention on her. "Are you feeling better?"

Hattie twisted her fingers in the silky folds of her dress. "Not really. Would it be a big deal if I left? I thought I could do this, but I'm not ready to make small talk with all these people." She closed her eyes briefly. "It's too hard," she said, her voice barely a whisper.

Evan's lips twisted into something resembling to a sneer as he transferred his weight from one foot to the other. "Hattie, this is our engagement party. We haven't been here for an hour. It'd look bad. People would ask questions."

She bit her lower lip. "Just tell them I have the stomach flu."

His hands curled into fists. "My mom worked really hard on this party. She'll be disappointed if you leave this early. I'll be disappointed." His eyes hardened. "You promised to try harder," he said through gritted teeth.

"Excuse me," I said, barely containing the anger pulsing through my veins. I couldn't believe Evan had the nerve to guilt her into staying after everything he'd done to her. He handed her to the

Vargas Cartel on a silver platter. He was complicit in the destruction of her life. "I think I should go. I don't want to interfere."

"Evan," Senator Deveron called from the hall. "Can you come here for a minute? I want you to meet someone."

"Sure." Evan tipped his head toward the ceiling. "Hattie, I have to talk to him. Join me in the entryway in a few minutes." He didn't wait for her to respond.

"Can you meet me this week?" I asked the minute Evan disappeared around the corner.

"I'm sorry, Ryker, but I can't." She shook her head. "It's not a good idea."

"You said you missed me. Was that a lie?" My voice was intentionally soft, but it didn't mask the anger burning beneath the surface. Rationally, I understood why she didn't want to meet me. I knew what I did to her. If she stopped to think about it for a second and pushed all of her emotions aside, she'd run from Evan and me.

"No," she snapped. "But I need some space. I'm confused. I don't understand why you're here—"

"Because I was invited," I retorted, curling my hands into fists at my sides.

"Exactly. Why the hell were you invited to my engagement party? Why the hell do you have two names? Why the hell are you in the United States? None of this makes sense."

"I'll explain all of it later." I kept my voice perfectly smooth and controlled. I didn't know what I'd tell her. It couldn't be the whole truth. I wanted to keep her sheltered from the reality of the way my world worked.

"Later?" She scoffed. "Just like you explained everything that happened in Mexico."

I winced inwardly. "No. I'll tell you everything I can." I always added a qualifier to my answers. In my line of work, it was a necessary evil. I envied people who inhabited the world of black and white. I lived in a world colored with a thousand shades of gray. A world where black was white, and white was black. Hattie would never understand.

"I've heard that before." Her golden eyes narrowed briefly. "I know what that means. You won't tell me a damn thing."

I couldn't force this right now. She needed time to process everything. I plucked my wallet from my back pocket and handed her a business card. "Call me when you're ready to talk."

She glared at the card, and for a minute, I didn't think she'd take it. "I'll think about," she said, ripping the card out of my hand and crumbling it inside of her fist.

"You do that." I crossed the study, my leather loafers echoing on the herringbone wood floor. Everything about Senator Deveron's house screamed of pretentious elegance. Crystals dripped from oversized chandeliers. Pristine white wood paneling covered the walls. A spiral staircase with a sweeping gilded railing greeted guests in the entry. It was all very Vegas, which was fitting. That's where he got his start. He owned a casino in Las Vegas before the people of Nevada elected him to be their Senator. Too bad the tentacles of the criminal underworld were firmly embedded in

Senator Deveron. He voted in accordance with their interests rather than those of his constituents. "But if you take too long, I'll come find you."

"What's that supposed to mean?"

I winked. "You know exactly what it means. We've been down this road many times before."

Chapter Six

Hattie

"Vera," I sighed as I stood up from the table and I wrapped my arms around her.

I invited her to lunch this afternoon. After weeks of avoiding her, I finally decided enough was enough.

I expected to see her at my engagement party two days ago, but she was noticeably absent. Clearly, my mom had a firm hand in the invitation process and neglected to invite her. She never liked my best friend.

At first, I was pissed at my mom, but then I realized it was my fault Vera didn't receive an invitation to the party. I'd spent the last few weeks wallowing in my personal pity party, which gave my mom the opening she needed to sink her claws into my life again. I'd worked hard over the last six years to forge my own path. I couldn't stand the thought of everything I'd done crumbling because I'd lost the will to fight for myself.

The meddling in my life had to stop, which

meant I had to take control and stop being a victim. This morning, I exercised for the first time since I had returned from Mexico, and now was going to eat lunch with my best friend. Just those simple steps made me feel more like myself than I had in weeks. I had a plan. I had a schedule. I would be okay. I could do this.

"I'm so mad at you," she declared as she returned my hug.

"I know. I'm a shitty friend. I don't have a good excuse for avoiding you." I released her and took a step back, a faint smile on my face.

She waved her hand at me, dismissing my comment. "I can't hold it against you. I can't even imagine what you've been through over the last two months. One minute you were talking to that guy, and thirty minutes later, I couldn't find you. I scoured that bar and every bar within walking distance until three in the morning. Eventually, I went back to the hotel."

"I know. I'm sure you were losing your mind. I'm sorry I put you through that." I settled into my chair at the table.

Vera slipped into the seat across from me. She eyed me warily for a few prolonged seconds. I focused on anything and nothing to avoid the intensity of her stare. With trembling hands, I lifted my napkin and placed it on my lap, taking far too long to arrange it.

She cleared her throat and planted her elbows on the edge of the table. "Do you want to talk about what happened?" She sucked her raspberry-stained lower lip into her mouth. "I'm fine either way. You can tell me everything, nothing, or a little bit in between."

My stomach twisted. I missed Vera. She accepted me without judgment. I shouldn't have waited so long to talk to her. I needed her, and I needed our friendship, particularly now. "How much do you know?"

"Not a lot. I called your dad the next afternoon when I realized you weren't coming back."

My eyes flared. "I can't imagine that conversation went over very well."

She shook her head. "No, it didn't. He freaked. After that day, your dad called me twice. The first time he told me you'd been abducted, and the second time he told me they had successfully negotiated your release. He didn't give me any details. Nobody knows anything. Evan hasn't breathed a word to his friends either."

"You asked them?"

She twisted a strand of her long red hair around her finger. "Of course."

"I thought you hated them."

"I did. I still do." She took a sip of ice water. "They didn't know anything except that you and Evan are back together." Her eyes narrowed. "Is that true?"

I shifted in my seat. Then, I exhaled and held out my hand. Sunlight bounced off my engagement ring. "Actually, we're engaged."

Her eyes flickered to the two-carat square diamond ring glittering on my finger. "Oh, I didn't realize. Nobody told me."

"I'm sorry I didn't mention it earlier. I should

have told you immediately."

She shrugged her shoulders, but it looked robotic…forced. "This is the first time we've talked other than by text. I understand." Her eyes darted around the restaurant as she fiddled with the prongs of her fork. "Can I help with the engagement party?"

"Evan's parents hosted the engagement party two days ago. My mom handled the invitations."

Carefully avoiding my eyes, she nodded, accepting my excuse without complaint. She knew my mom wouldn't invite her, but it didn't nullify my behavior. I'd been a bad friend, and I wanted to make it up to her.

"Tell me about it. Was it nice?" she asked, but I could tell she didn't care about the answer. My inability to get my shit together hurt her. I'd alienated my only true friend.

I swallowed over the lump growing in my throat with alarming efficiency. "No," I admitted. "I hated it. I hated the flowers. I hated the food. I don't want to marry him."

Her eyes snapped to mine. "Why? What are you saying?"

"Evan was waiting for me when they released me—"

"Wait," she interrupted. "When who released you?"

I sucked in a weighted breath. "The Vargas Cartel. From what I pieced together, they abducted me as leverage to secure the release of Ignacio's son from a U.S. prison."

"Ignacio?"

"Ignacio is the head of the Vargas Cartel," I clarified. "I guess they'd been watching me for a while. As the attorney general, my dad can influence the pardon process. That's why they took me. They wanted to force the U.S. government to release Ignacio's son."

Vera's mouth opened and closed at least three times before she spoke. "Did they hurt you?"

I didn't know how to answer that question. People asked me that same question so many times in so many ways I'd lost count. She scanned my face looking for clues, or scars, or whatever people thought they could see.

My eyes dropped to my lap, and I brushed my hand over the faint pink scar on my neck. Ignacio had nicked my neck with a knife during a live video conference with Evan and his dad. Ignacio's assault scared me, but my relationship with Ryker damaged me deep down where Ignacio never could. He made me want him. Crave him. Need him.

I smirked, but the action felt forced and unnatural. "I'm still alive. That's all that matters."

"Have you told anyone what happened?"

I shook my head, trying to erase the conflicting emotions, rising like a tidal wave from my gut. "No."

"Do you want to tell me what happened?" She placed her hand on the base of her throat, her green eyes suspiciously glossy. "I won't judge you or think differently of you. No matter what happened or what you did to survive, you'll always be my best friend. I promise."

"I know you wouldn't judge me, but I'm not

ready to talk about it." I waved away the waitress as she approached our table. I needed to ask Vera something before I lost my nerve. "Right now I need something else from you."

"What's that?"

I cast a glance around the restaurant, making sure I didn't know any of the other patrons. I selected a little-known restaurant, but my family and Evan's family had a large circle of acquaintances. I needed to be careful. I didn't want any of this to get back to Evan before I had a chance to talk to him. "Can I move into your apartment?"

"Of course," she responded without hesitation. "You're always welcome to stay with me. You're my best friend."

Smiling, I tucked a strand of hair behind my ear. "It's only temporary until I find an alternative, but I need to get out of Evan's apartment, and I can't go home. My mom is determined to see me marry Evan. She won't stop."

She scooted to the edge of her chair. "Are you going to break off your engagement?"

"Yes. I can't marry him. I think I'm in love with someone else." I cringed inwardly, and I lowered my gaze, afraid to see her reaction. In all honesty, I didn't know what I felt for Ryker. Part of me suspected I could love Ryker. He made my blood sing and my body hum. The other part of me believed our connection revolved around sex, and not even sex wrapped in a nice, neat bow with the façade of romance and sweet murmurings.

"Hold on." She waved her hand, and the corners of her eyes crinkled as she scrunched her face in surprise. "I think I missed something. Who do you *think* you're in love with?"

"This is the part I don't want to talk about." My eyes flickered to the side, avoiding eye contact as my insides flamed with shame and more than a little uncertainty. I took a bite of the crusty bread, but it stuck in my throat. "I can't talk about it. Not yet." I looked at her, silently pleading with her to understand. "Okay?"

Her lips puckered like she sucked a lemon. "I don't like this, Hattie. I don't like this at all."

My throat convulsed as I swallowed. "You don't have to like it. I don't like it either, but I need your support."

"What kind of support?"

"A two-week date with your air mattress, maybe less. That's it. I can't live with Evan while I sort out what's going on inside my head. He keeps pushing me for more, and I can't give him anything right now or ever."

She rubbed her temples, studying me without comment. Then, she reached across the table and gently squeezed my hand. It felt like the vice grip had loosened around my heart. I made another step in the right direction. I was taking control of my future...my life.

"Okay," she whispered. "But I'm only doing this because I don't want you to end up miserable and married to Evan or his clone."

"Neither do I." Unfortunately, I didn't know if choosing Ryker would make me happy either, but I knew Evan wouldn't. "Somebody once warned me not to settle for mediocrity while I still had the ability to chase my dreams."

Vera raised her eyebrows, her face lit up with interest. "Who told you that?"

I tapped my fingers on the table, debating what to tell her. I went with the truth. "Ignacio Vargas."

Chapter Seven

Ryker

I threw my phone onto my kitchen counter. Not only did I have to deal with Rever's non-stop grousing about finding a way to smuggle his pregnant girlfriend out of Mexico, but Hattie hadn't called me in the seven days since her engagement party. I didn't want to push too hard, but I would if necessary.

"What the fuck is wrong with you?" Rever sauntered out of my guest bedroom, looking nothing like his usually polished self. When did he shower last? His dark hair hung in clumps, sticking to the side of his face. His stubble had officially turned into a beard a few days ago, and dark circles shadowed his eyes.

"Can't you buy your own clothes?" Rever didn't hesitate to make himself at home in my apartment. He wore my clothes. He ate my food. He drove my car. "What's next? Are you going to borrow my toothbrush?" I barked, motioning to my jeans and worn black t-shirt.

"Fuck you. I don't like doing laundry and I don't have any money. Ignacio canceled my credit cards and closed my bank accounts."

"How did he do that? Don't you have passwords?"

Rever snorted. "You can do anything in Mexico when you have money."

I smirked. "Right. How could I forget?"

Mexico suffered from a culture of systemic bribery. One summer while staying with my dad, I decided I wanted a Mexican driver's license. I slipped the government clerk ten dollars. I bypassed the written exam and walked out with a license ten minutes later. The same thing happened every time a police officer pulled me over for a traffic violation.

I opened the refrigerator and snagged a beer. "Do you want one?"

"No. I don't drink."

My brows furrowed. "Since when?"

Rever rocked back on his heels. "Since I met Anna. She doesn't like it when I drink."

"What about drugs?" I said under my breath.

"I stopped taking those too."

I studied him, inspecting his body language for any indication he was lying to me. *Interesting*. He looked sincere. This had to be a first. The Rever from my childhood was a sarcastic asshole who only told the truth when it helped him. Maybe the month he spent in prison had changed him for the better. Regardless, I didn't have any intention of fully lowering my guard around him. After all, Ignacio groomed him, and Ignacio was a master manipulator. A Machiavellian strategist.

"Have you talked to Anna?"

"I just hung up with her." He looked pained.

I raised my eyebrows. "And?"

"There's no way she can make it to that tunnel in Sonora. Her dad has relocated her to the house on Isla Mujeres. He thinks the Vargas Cartel plans to hurt her."

I exhaled loudly, hanging my head in my hands. "Maybe she should come clean and explain her situation. It might be the only option. I'm not going to break into a house on that island. I wouldn't walk out of there alive. Neither of us would. It would be a death march."

Isla Mujeres was a four-mile island located off the coast of Cancun, Mexico. Smuggling someone from that island would be a logistical nightmare. There wasn't a quick getaway plan.

Rever punched the wall. It echoed through my apartment like a gunshot, and drywall dust coated his knuckles. "We have to try. I'm not going to abandon her and my unborn child."

I chuckled even as my blood boiled. I didn't owe Rever shit. I already saved him from himself once. I didn't need to do it again. I sympathized with Anna. I wished the reality of the situation were different. "This is your mess. I don't have time for this right now."

Rever rose to his full height, squared his shoulders, and cocked his head. "If we don't help her, they'll kill her. Are you okay with them killing your unborn niece or nephew?"

"Now you want to claim me as part of your

family?" My voice dripped with derision. I raked my hand across my chest. "You have some fucking nerve pulling the family card now." As kids, Rever never missed an opportunity to tell me I wasn't part of his family. That I'd never be part of his real family. According to him, we shared blood, but nothing else.

"You're all I have." He had this hopeless, hollow look in his eyes full of fear, fear of the unknown, and fear of the known. I knew that look. That's how I felt when I threw Hattie out of my life and back into Evan's open arms. I fucking hated that prick.

Gritting my teeth, I clenched my hand around my beer bottle so hard my knuckles whitened. My phone—the one reserved strictly for business of Ryker Vargas, not Ry Fallon—rang, saving me from answering. Only past and potential clients had the number. I slipped the phone out of my pocket. "I need to take this call."

Rever briefly closed his eyes, then he rolled his shoulders back and retreated to my guest bedroom. I couldn't get him away from me and out of my life fast enough.

"Ryker Vargas," I said, my voice clipped.

"It's Senator Deveron."

I didn't say anything for a moment. I had no intention of doing jobs for him anymore, but refusing a job from him wouldn't be easy.

"How can I help you?"

Labored breathing hummed in my ear. "We have a problem."

"Really? How do you figure?"

"Hattie broke off the engagement with Evan."

My heart stalled in my chest, and then it started beating riotously. *Thank God.* "Sounds like Evan has a problem, not me. I completed the job. I've been paid. We're done."

"Hm." Papers rustled in the background and then he sighed. "I heard Rever slipped back into the U.S. In fact, all the evidence suggests he's hiding out in D.C. I don't have his exact location, but it's only a matter of time."

Dammit. I should've shown my brother to the door the minute I saw him in my apartment. Better yet, I should've called Ignacio and asked him to forcibly drag his ass back to Mexico. Senator Deveron had all the leverage he needed to involve me in a new scheme. For some reason, the Senator had continued nosing around the Vargas Cartel and me, both as Ryker and Ry. It was making me uneasy. Hell, everything was making me uneasy these days.

I was playing with fire. I had enough experience with backroom deals and shady undertakings to know something bad was going to happen, but I didn't know if there was a damned thing I could do to stop it.

"That's news to me," I lied as a thousand curses poured like liquid through my mind.

Strained seconds passed, each one more intense than the previous one.

"I wouldn't want Rever to be picked up by the FBI or immigration. We'd be right back where we started. Rever in jail. Evan and Hattie separated," Senator Deveron said.

I took a long draw of my beer. "I don't give a

fuck about the status of Evan and Hattie's relationship. It sounds like Evan can't seal the deal. Maybe you should be calling him instead of me."

"You should care."

"Why's that?" I asked, even though my experience told me I shouldn't say a thing. Asking questions gave the appearance I cared. It was a sign of weakness.

"It's common knowledge the Alvarez and Vargas cartels are at war right now."

"What's your point? A cartel war is hardly a novel event. Over a hundred thousand people have died in the last decade as a result of cartel-related violence in Mexico."

"Yet, the Vargas Cartel has been largely immune from all the death and destruction. Have you ever wondered why?"

"Please enlighten me," I quipped.

He chuckled. "Over the last five years, U.S. enforcement agencies have protected the Vargas Cartel in exchange for information about rival drug gangs. We've provided weapons. We helped him launder money, and we turned a blind eye to his smuggling activities."

"And in exchange, the Vargas Cartel opened its war chest and funded all your campaigns. You basically made the U.S. government an accessory to all sorts of criminal behavior." I had gleaned most of this information from undercover operatives and Ignacio, but I couldn't believe Senator Deveron openly admitted the connection. Even after the Fast and Furious scandal revealed the ATF had sold guns to drug cartels, the media ignored the U.S.

government's symbiotic relationship with Mexican drug cartels.

"Exactly. We have a mutually beneficial relationship. Can you imagine what would happen to your family if the U.S. government shifted its protection to the Alvarez Cartel? With Rever out of the picture, they're already missing a successor. How long do you think it would take before the members of the Vargas Cartel defected and joined ranks with the Alvarez Cartel?"

I laughed coldly, even as my gut twisted into knots thinking about the implications of his threat. "Maybe I don't give a shit." It was an outright lie. As much as I wanted to sever my ties to the Vargas Cartel, I didn't want my dad to die, and that's exactly what would happen if Senator Deveron made good on his threat. My dad wasn't a good man, but I loved him. I didn't want anything to happen to him.

"We both know that's not true."

"I don't see how I can help you."

"Threaten her. Threaten her family. Hold a gun to her head. Blackmail her. I don't care. Get it done. That's what you do. That's why I hired you."

"Blackmail her?" I said, barely able to form the words. Rage whipped through my veins like an electrical storm. If he knew about the video of Hattie and me together, I'd kill Ignacio. I owed him some degree of loyalty, but my loyalty stopped the minute he threatened Hattie. "With what?"

"Everybody has secrets. Find hers."

I paced back and forth, squeezing my phone hard enough to shatter it into a million pieces. Before I met Hattie, I wouldn't have wavered for a second. As much as I despised the family business, I never would've chosen anyone or anything to the detriment of my family. Now I was walking the tightrope to hell. "I'll think about it."

"What does that mean?" Senator Deveron spat.

"That I'll call you in the next seventy-two hours and not a minute earlier." I disconnected the call.

"Shit. Shit. Shit," I screamed as I flung my empty beer bottle at the wall.

Chapter Eight

Hattie

I jogged on the paved path next to the Potomac River. I loved this time of year. Pink cherry blossoms splashed color across the normally staid D.C. landscape, making it lighter, happier.

Over the last seven days, I had reclaimed my life and future. I still missed Ryker, Ry, or whoever the hell he was, but I needed to move forward instead of backward.

I had broken off my engagement with Evan. Less than five minutes into the conversation, Evan went from compassionate boyfriend to complete jackass. Every cutting comment he tossed in my direction only solidified my decision to walk away from that part of my life and carve a new future.

I stopped by my parents' house three days ago to give them the news. I thought my mom's head was going explode or spin in circles when I told her, but my dad understood and agreed with my decision. So did my therapist, which I pointed out to my mom on a daily basis. She hadn't abandoned her mission to convince me to marry Evan, but the frequency of her comments had decreased, which was fine...for now.

I salvaged my friendship with Vera. In fact, she offered to clean out her guest bedroom and make our roommate situation permanent. As much as I loved living with her, I hadn't decided either way. I wanted to keep my options open and make the right decision instead of jumping into anything like I did with Evan and the engagement.

My professors and I agreed on a path that would allow me to complete the requirements for my graduate degree by the end of the summer.

Finally, I had resumed my exercise schedule. I jogged instead of swam. Swimming laps reminded me of Mexico, which reminded me of Ryker. I didn't have a plan to deal with him yet. Maybe he'd just disappear again, and I'd never have to come to terms with whatever happened between us.

Despite my determination to avoid him, he still managed to consume my thoughts. Somehow he had charmed his way into my heart. The minute his lips touched mine at the engagement party, my body melted into his, and all my hard-fought defenses crumbled. Time fragmented, giving the illusion not a minute had passed since we were together.

I rounded the corner of the park, my feet slapping against the paved path, echoing in my ears with every stride. Too quickly, the timer buzzed on my phone, signaling the end of my run. Endorphins flooded my veins, making me wish I could keep going until I couldn't think about anything but the next step, the next mile, and the burning in my lungs. Maybe next time.

Right now, I needed to keep my schedule. My schedule would keep me sane, focused even. Before the Vargas Cartel abducted me, I had planned every minute of every day. It gave me control of my life, something I never had as a child.

My chest heaving, I bent at the waist, bracing my hands on my knees. When my heart slowed to a normal pace, I walked to the bench where I stretched after every run for ten minutes before I drove home.

I froze mid-stride. Ryker sat five feet in front of me on *my* bench.

Shit.

My endorphins evaporated like dry ice. Why couldn't he leave me alone? Why did he keep interfering in my life? I needed my routine. It kept me grounded...in control. I glanced over my shoulder as I backpedaled a few clumsy steps.

"You can run away, but it'd be a waste of time." He stood and sauntered to me, his shoes crunching over the gravel.

I planted my hands on my hips and cocked my chin, feigning composure, even as my heart jack-knifed painfully in my chest. Over a week had passed without hearing from him or seeing him. I thought my craving for him had faded. The razor-sharp ache in my chest told me otherwise. "Why's that?"

He came to a stop less than a foot in from of me, running his thumb and index finger along his scruffy jaw line. His proximity unsettled me in too many ways to count. God, he looked amazing. I wanted to touch him, taste him, and slip my hands under his black shirt.

"I'll follow you."

I squeezed the bridge of my nose. "I don't have time for this. I have plans."

His metallic gray eyes narrowed, a confusing complexity of emotions swirling in his eyes. "Where are you headed?"

"It's none of your business, but I need to stop by my professor's office to pick up some books." I raised one eyebrow and smiled. "I had to drop my classes since I missed nearly a month of school, but I'd still like to graduate by the end of the summer."

"I'll join you."

"Do I have a choice?"

He smirked. "No."

I rolled my eyes even as my skin trembled with awareness and my heart bled with a ruthless concoction of anxiety and lust. "Glad to see some things never change."

A jumbled mess of disjointed thoughts twisted through my mind as Ryker and I strolled to my car in silence, neither of us making any attempt at conversation. Words weren't needed. We both knew he could force me to go with him. We played this game in Mexico many times. I didn't need a refresher. It should frighten me to be alone with him, especially when I had started to rebuild my life again. Too bad I was powerless to resist him.

Powerless because of my attraction to him.

Powerless because we both knew he could overpower me…make me do what he wanted.

Powerless because I'd never stop wanting him.

I pulled my key out of my pocket, but he grabbed my hand. I frowned. "What?"

"We're taking my car." He snagged the key, stuffed it in his pocket, and pointed to the black Mercedes Sedan parallel parked in front of my car.

"No thanks. I'll follow you," I hissed.

He smirked as he brushed the back of his knuckles along my face. I ignored the tingle down my spine and the pebbling of my nipples. It didn't mean anything. It was a chemical reaction, nothing more.

"Nice try. You're driving with me. We have things to discuss," he murmured, the corners of his eyes crinkling like he found me utterly amusing.

I folded my arms across my chest and shook my head. "No, we don't."

He leaned his hip against his car. "Please, Hattie."

I wanted to yell at him, fight him. Then, he cracked open the passenger door of his car. I stared at him, unmoving for a few beats. For weeks, I wanted nothing more than to spend time with him. To talk to him. To be near him. Now, I had the chance.

"Fine," I mumbled. No matter the emotional distance I erected between us, it disintegrated whenever I saw him.

He tucked my seatbelt around my body and fastened it. "Here," he said, holding out my key.

"You're already giving it back?"

The corner of his lips quirked up almost imperceptibly. "I don't want you to feel like a prisoner."

"Thanks," I whispered. I sucked air into my nose as his car pulled away from the curb and into the early afternoon traffic.

"Talk," I said after three minutes as I tapped my fingers on my leg. The anticipation of our conversation was killing me, second-by-second, minute-by-minute. His smell surrounded me, slowly driving me crazy with each inhalation. I scoured my mind trying to remember all the reasons I shouldn't want him, but none of them seemed to matter when I was with him.

"I heard you broke off your engagement to Evan." It was a statement, not a question.

"So?" Heat flooded my face. I didn't want him to think I did it because he told me to.

"Why?"

"Because I don't like him. I won't marry him. I'd rather be alone."

"You need to get back together with him."

I whipped my head toward him. *What the hell?* "Excuse me. Did you just tell me to get back together with Evan?"

"Yes. That's exactly what you're going to do, preferably this afternoon. The sooner, the better." He didn't sound like Ryker. His voice was clipped, cool, and polite, like we were complete strangers. Ice crept through my veins. He subjected me to his sudden mood changes too often in Mexico, and I was sick of them.

"You're giving me whiplash. A week ago you kissed me and told me to break off my engagement, and now you're telling me to crawl back to him." I pointed at him, my finger trembling. "Well, fuck you. I don't want Evan. I never will." I swept the sweaty strands of hair away from my face. "And you know what? I don't want you either. Leave me alone. I'm done being a pawn in this fucked up game."

All the emotions taunting me for the last few weeks bubbled to the surface, and I was livid. I had enough. I wanted to tear my hair out, beat my chest, or throw a tantrum worthy of a two year old—anything to stop the madness clamoring inside my head. As his car slowed to a stop at a traffic light, I reached for the door handle.

"Don't even think about it." He yanked my hand away from the door. "This conversation isn't over."

"Guess what?" I taunted, my nostrils flaring. I felt like my head would explode any second as rage burned through my veins. "This isn't Mexico. We're not in the middle of the jungle. The Vargas Cartel doesn't have any power here, so stop telling me what to do."

"Dammit." He slammed his hand against the steering wheel. "This isn't a joke, Hattie. You have to get back together with him."

"Tell me why?"

"I can't—"

"Of course not. Why would things change now? Why would anyone give me answers? Is this some sick and twisted game? Fuck with Hattie until she checks herself into a mental hospital."

He cocked his head to the side. "No. I'm still trying to protect you." He lowered his voice. "I'm always trying to protect you."

"If this is how you protect me, I'd hate to know

what it feels like when you stop." I dropped my head into my hands. "Do you know what I've gone through since I got home? Do you have any idea?"

"Hattie," he said, his voice soft. "I'm sorry it has to be this way. I'm sorry about everything. If I could change what happened to you, I would."

Acid seared the walls of my throat, making it hard to breathe. "I've lost control of my life, and it kills me. I hate myself. I hate who I've become. And you know the icing on the cake in this whole fucked up charade?" He shook his head. "Until last week, I thought I was pregnant. Can you imagine what a fucking disaster that would've been? I still haven't had my period."

"Pregnant?" he said, his voice distant and threaded with frost.

"Yeah, pregnant. In case you've already forgotten the details, we didn't use protection."

"I didn't think—"

"Right. You didn't think. I didn't think. That's the point. Neither of us was thinking. In fact, nobody is thinking about what's good for me anymore. They only care about how they look and what they want." I white-knuckled the side of my seat, squeezing so hard; I was surprised my fingernails didn't puncture the buttery leather. "Evan thinks I'm being selfish. My mom thinks I need to honor my commitment to Evan. You think I should get back together with Evan. Fuck, even Senator Deveron called to tell me he thinks I'm behaving impulsively."

He turned off the car ignition, and I stared out the window, studying the gray walls of the parking garage.

"Hattie."

"Leave me alone," I said without heat because I was tired. Tired of my life. Tired of this back and forth. So tired I could feel the bags growing under my eyes. "Please. I can't do this anymore."

He grabbed my hand. "Look at me."

"What?" I turned to look at him. Was that regret or exasperation lurking behind his hooded gray eyes?

"You're right."

Glaring at him, I asked, "Right about what?"

"Everything. Nobody has considered you in this whole mess, including me, and I'm sorry about that." He combed his hands through his inky black hair and shifted his gaze forward. The overhead parking garage lamp lit up one side of his face, half dark, half-light, just like Ryker. "You don't have to get back together with Evan. I'll find another way."

My brows furrowed. "You'll find another way?" I echoed. "Another way to do what?"

Need and tenderness were etched into the hard angles of his face. Ryker brushed a thumb over my lips, and my lungs constricted. "To do my job and still keep you safe."

"I don't like this, Ryker. What aren't you telling me?"

A smile tugged at his lips and his eyes glowed. He was so close I could see the fiery yellow flecks around his pupils. "Lots of things. Too many things." He opened the car door. "Let's go. You have a schedule to keep."

I scowled, and he rubbed the back of his hand

across his lips, smothering his laugh. It didn't work.
"Do I amuse you?"
    "Always."

Chapter Nine

Ryker

I held Hattie's hand as we wove through the throngs of people rushing to class on the University campus. She talked about her passion for politics and her plans to take make-up classes this summer. I nodded and smiled where appropriate, but I couldn't form the words to respond.

Guilt coated my stomach. I couldn't believe I had asked her to reconcile with Evan. Sleep eluded me last night as I explored my options. In the end, I had decided to sacrifice Hattie, at least temporarily, until I figured out another solution.

I didn't deserve her. She deserved someone better. Someone without baggage. Someone not tainted by lies. Unfortunately for her, I was selfish, and I had no intention of letting her go. Ever. I couldn't imagine not wanting her.

"We're going in there." She pointed at a cream-colored structure. "This is the library. I need to grab a few books I have on reserve. Then, we can go."

"I'll wait here."

She startled as I ran the pad of my fingertips down the side of her face to her collarbone. The air crackled with static electricity. Shifting on her feet, she bit down on her lower lip. She was nervous. I made her nervous.

She lowered her gaze. "Okay. It should only take me a few minutes."

A smile spread across my face, and I yanked her against me, keeping our hands entwined. She curled her free hand around my shoulder, and it was all the permission I needed. I didn't know how many more chances Hattie would give me, but I refused to let one slip away.

I covered her mouth with a searing kiss, conquering her sweet taste one stroke and slide at a time. Her body swayed into mine as her fingers tangled in my hair. My heart pounded in unison with hers. Urgency roared through my blood as our last night together flickered through my mind. The memory of that night had haunted me for weeks—the feel of her silken skin against my fingertips, the taste of her lips, her fresh, crisp scent, and everything uniquely Hattie. I wanted to feel her body beneath mine again as I took everything she had to offer and more.

Then, all too quickly she pulled her head back. Hattie gaped at me with a mixture of wonder and fear; her pleasure-stung lips parted as her fingertips stroked my jaw line.

"Hattie," I muttered. "I've tried to let you go over and over in Mexico and again today. But this is it. I'm done trying."

Her eyes glistened. "Ryker, I want this to work,

but I don't know if I'm ready. I need to sort through all these messy emotions I have for you."

I raised an eyebrow. "What do you mean?"

"This morning I had convinced myself I felt attached to you because of our twisted history and everything would fade. But when I see you…" She shook her head and exhaled a delicate puff of air. "When we're alone, everything changes. There's just something about you, about us, that makes me want to take a chance. That may make me an idiot, but maybe I don't care anymore."

"I have an idea," I rasped.

She smiled as her hand toyed with the top button of my shirt, and I groaned inwardly. "Yeah?"

"Come out to dinner with me tomorrow."

"How's that going to solve anything?"

"It will give us time together in a normal setting, without worrying about life or death or the Vargas Cartel."

The corners of her lips curled upward. "What's this really about? Why are you suddenly back in my life?"

"I'm not done with whatever happened between us, and I don't think you are either." I waved my hand back and forth between our bodies. "I think we should explore this. See where it goes. See if it's real."

Her mood lifted. "I'd like that."

I brushed a quick kiss across her lips. "Go. I have to make a call. Meet me at the car."

Her eyes narrowed. "Okay."

She jogged up the front steps of the library. The minute the door closed behind her, I pulled my phone out of my pocket.

"Senator Deveron, it's Ryker Vargas. Is now a good time to talk?"

"One minute." A door slammed. "You're calling earlier than I anticipated. I guess that means you have good news."

"It depends on your definition of good news," I hedged. "Good news for me or good news for you."

"Which is it?" he asked through gritted teeth.

I laughed coldly. "Good news for me."

"Explain."

"Did you know Ignacio is a meticulous record keeper? He records every conversation. He documents every bribe, political donation, and every favor or slight."

"No." He cleared his throat. "He's never told me that."

"I didn't think so, because if you knew, you wouldn't be threatening the Vargas Cartel. If the Vargas Cartel goes down, we'll take you with us. Consider this your one and only warning."

"And if I don't heed your warning?"

"Did you hear about the politician in Monterrey who was killed after crossing the Vargas Cartel?"

"I don't know what you're talking about." His voice fractured on the last word.

"Well, let me enlighten you. They draped his skinned face over a statue of a Mexican golden eagle on the front steps of City Hall. Alongside the statute were two garbage bags. One contained his torso and the other contained his legs, arms, and scalped skull."

"What the hell are you trying to tell me?"

"*VC captura y exucutes traidores,*" I hissed, saying the words I hadn't uttered in more than a decade, not since I watched Ignacio's personal hit team lodge fifty knives in a man. It was the Vargas Cartel's calling card. Every cartel had one. "The Vargas Cartel captures and executes traitors," I said, repeating the words in English.

"Are you threatening me?"

"Yes."

"You'll never get close enough to me to do a damn thing," he snapped.

"Maybe not, but I won't have any trouble getting close to Evan or your wife."

He sucked in a breath. "What's wrong with you? Don't threaten my family."

"You threatened mine. I'm returning the favor," I shot back. I might even carry out the threat myself, and if I shared his threats with Ignacio, he wouldn't hesitate either. Ignacio didn't rise to the top of the Vargas Cartel by exercising mercy. Senator Deveron underestimated us if he thought we'd roll over and cower to his threats.

Senator Deveron's heavy breaths echoed through the phone. "What do you want?"

"I want you to stay out of cartel business, and I want you to stay the fuck out of Hattie Covington's life."

"Whose side are you on?"

"Mine. Always mine," I snapped.

He blew out a steady stream of air. "It's in the Vargas Cartel's best interest if she marries Evan. We need Hattie's dad on our side. If an investigation lands on his desk, he has prosecutorial discretion not to pursue the matter."

I flung my car door open and slid inside. "He won't be attorney general forever. You're going to need to find a more permanent way to secure your political legacy and keep your ass out of jail. One that doesn't involve Hattie Covington."

"Why the sudden interest in her? Why are you protecting her?"

Fuck. I had tipped my hand. Senator Deveron might be careless, but he wasn't dumb. "Because the Vargas Cartel doesn't hurt innocent women." Unlike other cartels, the Vargas Cartel had a code of ethics. It didn't hurt women. It didn't kill innocent people. It didn't assassinate people for money. It only killed people who deserved to die. Ignacio bent the rules with Hattie, but at the time, Ignacio was desperate to secure Rever's release.

My message delivered, I disconnected the call. We didn't have anything else to discuss, not right then. I wouldn't fool myself. That wasn't the end of Senator Deveron and his threats. He'd be back, but I'd be ready. If it meant I had to destroy his political career and sell his secrets to the highest bidder, I would.

Chapter Ten

Hattie

By six o'clock in the evening, I was officially a nervous wreck. I had plans to meet Ryker at a restaurant in a half hour. He wanted to pick me up, but I refused. I didn't know if Vera would recognize him, but I refused to take the risk. Not yet anyway.

"I won't be too late," I said. I brushed my hands down the front of the form-fitting red dress I paired with nude-colored heels and a nude-colored purse.

Vera folded her arms across her chest. "Why isn't your date picking you up here?"

I cracked the seal on the front door. "Because I didn't want him to." We'd already had a variation of this conversation three times in the last hour.

She rolled her eyes and flipped her braid over her shoulder. "So you keep telling me." She leaned her back against the kitchen counter and took a sip of her wine. "But you still won't tell my why."

"It's not important."

Her lips pressed into a tight line as she looked between the door and me. "If you're concerned...I mean, if you think I'll judge you, you're wrong."

I glanced longingly at the traffic clogging the street. I wished I could slip out the door and end this conversation once and for all. "It's not that."

"Then what is it?"

"I would rather meet him at the restaurant. I don't want him in this part of my life…yet."

"But what if something happens?" she protested, shaking her head back and forth. "I won't have any information." Her voice wavered, and unshed tears glistened in the corners of her eyes.

My lungs constricted. I knew what she meant. I understood her concerns. I disappeared once. She hadn't said as much, but she blamed herself. "I'll be fine. I promise." I sighed. "But just in case, I'm going to 902 Restaurant."

She bowed her head. "Thanks."

"You're welcome," I answered before I closed the door behind me. I lingered next to the front door for a moment before getting into the backseat of the cab waiting beside the curb.

Twenty minutes later, I walked into a small restaurant in the Cleveland Park area. Faint music hummed through the air. I scanned the room for Ryker. When my gaze landed on him, my breath caught in my throat, and my insides squeezed. Would I always react so forcefully to him?

My eyes singularly focused on him. I crossed the restaurant, my heels tapping on the hardwood floor. I paused when I reached the edge of his table. Ryker's eyes swept over my body from head to toe and back up again. A languid shiver traveled down my spine, tap-dancing on each of my vertebrae.

He stood and brushed a kiss across my lips. "You look beautiful. Good enough to eat."

I dipped my head, hiding a satisfied smile. This dress was way out of my comfort zone, but I mentally patted myself on the back for wearing it. "Thanks. You don't look so bad yourself." He wore a white collared shirt with a steely gray suit. The combination made his eyes look almost silver. "No black tonight?"

He chuckled, and his warm breath tickled the side of my face. "No." He pulled out the chair directly across from him. "Please, sit."

We settled into our seats. Almost immediately, I felt on edge. I didn't know how to talk to Ryker in a normal setting. We'd been intimate. I killed a man for him. He killed three men for me, yet we didn't know much about each other. I twisted my hands in my lap.

"Relax," he said.

"I am relaxed."

"You're fidgeting."

"Fine." I place my hand on the edge of the table. "Is this better?"

He nodded. "Why are you nervous?"

I swallowed hard as I scanned the restaurant décor, purposely avoiding his gaze. "I don't know what to talk about."

"What do you want to know about me?" he countered.

"You'll tell me anything?"

"Sure, I'll tell you everything I can without endangering you."

I rolled my eyes. "So how'd things go with

Rever?"

His eyes narrowed briefly. "Rever? Why do you want to know about him?"

I shrugged. It seemed like a safe topic. "I don't know. I guess I'm curious what happened when he got home."

"Rever's living with me."

"Seriously? How'd that happen?"

"It's a long story, but basically Ignacio cut him off, and I was his last and only option."

Surprised, I raised my eyebrows. "How's that going? I didn't think you two were on the best terms."

"We still aren't. He wants my help with something."

I shifted to the edge of my seat. "Do you mind if I ask what he wants?"

He sighed wearily. "He wants me to smuggle his girlfriend out of Mexico."

"What?" I blurted out a little too loudly.

"She's Juan Alvarez's daughter."

My mind scrambled to place the name. "Who's that?"

"The head of the Alvarez Cartel." He tugged on the cuffs of his shirt. "Things haven't improved between the two cartels since you left."

I nodded. I hadn't kept up with current events since I came home. In fact, I refused to read a single article about Mexican drug cartels. After my stay at the Vargas compound in Mexico, the violence, death, and conflicts in the newspapers were all too real for my taste. "Are you going to do it?"

"Maybe," he answered evasively. "How do you

like living with Vera?" he asked, changing the direction of the conversation.

"It's much better than living with Evan."

He frowned. "What'd you tell her about us?"

"Nothing."

Ryker shot me a hard look. I didn't know if he disapproved, or he didn't believe me, but I didn't have time to question him. The waitress appeared. I hadn't looked at the menu, which didn't matter because Ryker ordered the tasting menu with the wine pairing. After she had taken our order, our conversation shifted to small talk about my plans to finish my graduate degree and his work as a campaign bundler.

"So what do you want to do when you graduate?"

I took a sip of my wine. "In a perfect world?"

He smiled. "Sure."

"I used to want to work for the United Nations." Now, I wasn't sure what I wanted. My old goals lost some of their appeal over the last two months.

He scoffed. "You can't be serious."

I leaned forward. "What's wrong with the UN?"

"Call me crazy, but there's something fundamentally wrong with an organization that allows countries with repeated human rights violations to sit on the Human Rights Council." I frowned. "Cuba, Saudi Arabia, Pakistan, China…just to name a few. There's nothing like an honor killing or imprisoning your political opposition that says we respect human rights."

"Well, it's a starting point to open discussions with those countries on human rights. You never know. They might change. Evolve."

"Unlikely."

"Hey, you're a campaign bundler. You shouldn't be so cynical about the political system."

"It's because of my profession that I'm cynical. Money and greed rule politics, not ideals and lofty visions of utopia."

"Maybe you're right," I conceded. "Lately, I've been rethinking my career choice."

"Why's that?" he asked with one eyebrow lifted.

"With my background and family, everyone assumed I'd pursue a career in politics, so that's the course I chose." I shrugged. "After everything I've gone through, I want to make sure I pursue my dream, not my mom or dad's dream."

"And you're not sure?"

"It's still up for debate."

***

By the time our dessert arrived, I was stuffed.

"I can't eat another bite. I'm done," I declared, leaning back in my chair.

The waitress placed the check on the corner of the table. "So where to now?"

"I'm going to use the bathroom, then home, I guess. Can you ask our waitress to call me a cab?"

"I'll take you home. It's bad enough you wouldn't let me pick you up."

"I don't think that's a good idea. Vera—"

"Not a problem. I won't get out of the car," he countered.

This was why dating Ryker would never work.

I'd always be wondering when someone would puzzle everything together. I glanced over my shoulder, gathering the courage to do what needed to be done. Dissolve all my ties to him once and for all.

My stomach plummeted along with all the blood in my head when my eyes connected with Evan's. "Oh shit," I whispered, abruptly severing eye contact. "We have to go."

Ryker followed my line of sight. Then, he grabbed my hand. "It'll be fine. Just act naturally. You're not doing anything wrong."

"But...But," I stammered.

He raised one eyebrow, searing me with his gunmetal gray eyes. "Hi, Evan," he said as he released my hand.

"Ry," Evan said through clenched teeth as he laser focused all his attention on me. "I didn't realize you were already dating other people. It's been what," he lifted one shoulder casually, "three or four days since you broke off our engagement?"

I bounced my leg up and down under the table. "That sounds about right."

Evan folded his arms across his chest. "I thought you needed space to figure out your life."

"I do," I snapped. "That's what I'm doing."

"Just tell me how long you waited."

I blinked. "How long I waited for what?"

Evan's eyes cut to Ryker. Then, he leaned forward, bracing his palms on the edge of our table. "Did you start fucking him immediately after our engagement party, or did you wait until we broke up?"

My eyes flared as I sucked in a breath, but I didn't get the opportunity to respond. Ryker jumped out of his chair and grabbed Evan by the collar of his shirt, yanking him forward so only inches separated their faces. "Apologize."

"Apologize?" Evan laughed bitterly, his face hard, his eyes dark and narrowed. "Why? She's the one who needs to apologize. She's the one who ended our engagement and moved on five seconds later."

Ryker's fist twisted in the fabric of Evan's shirt. "She's not your concern anymore."

Evan tried to grab my hand, but I lowered it to my lap and out of his reach. "I love you, Hattie. I stood by you. I accepted you back into my life. I didn't even make you explain anything. Is this how you repay me?"

I popped out of my chair, and it tumbled backward. He said those three words with conviction, but I didn't believe him. Not anymore. I saw a man who loved the idea of us, and what we could do together, but he didn't love me. "Accepted me back into your life? I didn't do anything wrong. I was a victim."

"Did you tell him what happened?" Evan asked, his eyes narrowed into dark slits.

Ryker released Evan's shirt. "I know everything," he said, answering the question for me.

"You hardly know him." Hurt flashed across Evan's face. "You told him, and you wouldn't tell me anything. Not a single fucking detail. Why? Don't you trust me?"

Guilt dissected my heart like a sword. "Evan," I

said, holding my hand over my chest. "Can we talk about this later? This isn't time or the place."

Evan surveyed the restaurant. Everyone was watching us with a mixture of horror and excitement. What a disaster. He squared his shoulders and took a few steps back. "You're right."

I nodded. "I'll call you soon, okay?"

Without responding, he spun around and headed to the entrance. He whispered something to a blonde woman in a short emerald green dress. Her eyes flashed to me. Then, Evan threaded his arm through hers, and they strolled out of the restaurant as though nothing had happened. I guess he could date, but I couldn't. Typical Evan logic. He had the audacity to accuse me of moving on too quickly and act as if I had wounded him when he brought a date too.

For a frozen eternity, I didn't have the energy to do anything. I exhaled shakily. Fatigue had settled into my bones, and I wanted to go home, climb into bed, and forget about everything…everyone. Tears beaded in the corners of my eyes, but I refused to cry over Evan. He had already claimed too much of my life and wasted too much of my time. I cleared my throat and shifted on my feet. "Well, that was awkward."

Ryker stared at me, the silence ballooning with every tick of the second hand, but I couldn't tear my eyes away from his. Then, his sensual lips curved into a smile, jumpstarting my heart. He chuckled under his breath as he slapped some money on top of the bill. "I think we outstayed our welcome. Let's get out of here."

His lips swept across mine, and his scent swaddled me, soothing my frayed nerves, uncoiling the tension holding my muscles hostage. "Tell me what you're thinking," he whispered.

"That I can't believe you wanted me to get back together with him."

Chapter Eleven

Ryker

"This looks amazing," Rever said, leaning over my shoulder.

"It's not for you," I said, elbowing him in his stomach.

Rever stumbled back. "What the hell?"

I turned off the stove and snagged my keys from the counter, stuffing them into my pocket. "You need to leave."

He leaned against the kitchen counter, his ankles crossed. "I don't have anywhere to go."

"Go out to dinner. Check into a hotel. I don't care. You can't stay here tonight."

"With what money?" he challenged.

I opened my wallet and pulled out five crisp hundred dollar bills. "Take this." I dropped the stack of bills on the counter.

Rever eyed the money, but didn't make any attempt to grab it. "No."

"We've already been over this. Hattie's coming over for dinner, and you can't be here."

"I'll stay in the guest room. She won't even know I'm here."

I groaned. "I'll know you're here."

"Look, Ryker, both of us know I shouldn't step foot out of your apartment. Senator Deveron knows I'm in D.C. He could have me picked up again, and then we'd be fucked. Anna would be fucked."

He was right. As much as I wanted him to leave, it wasn't a good decision for either of us. It'd been a week since we went out to dinner and ran into Evan. She hadn't mentioned him again, and I hadn't asked her any questions. I didn't want to push her. She'd let me back into her life, which was good enough for me. For now.

"Fine." I opened my front door. "I'll be back in ten minutes. Don't come out of the room tonight."

"Are you ever going to introduce us?"

"Not if I don't have to."

"So you're embarrassed by me." It wasn't a question.

"Pretty much," I answered, slamming the door behind me. Hattie and I managed to build some trust over the last week, but I didn't want to throw Rever in her face. Likewise, she didn't want to introduce me to her friends. Maybe someday we'd figure out how to incorporate our friends and family into our relationship, but right now I wanted to concentrate on us.

I jogged across the street. As usual, Hattie and I had planned to meet at the bar two blocks from my apartment. We'd been careful to avoid meeting in places where we could run into her friends or family.

I opened the door of the neighborhood bar. The smell of stale beer assaulted my nose. Dark wood covered the walls. I wove through the crowds of people taking advantage of the happy hour menu. My leather soles clicked over the gray and white checkerboard tile floor.

Hattie sat at a booth in the corner, twirling her fingers around the stem of a nearly empty glass of white wine. Her other hand tapped impatiently on the sleek and industrial-looking gunmetal tabletop. My late arrival didn't go unnoticed by her.

Like every other time we had met in the past week, I nodded to her, and then I walked directly through the bar to the back entrance. Normally, we walked the two blocks to my car and drove somewhere outside D.C., but tonight she was coming to my apartment for dinner.

"You're late." She circled her arms around my neck.

"Dinner complications." My gaze drifted to her lips. I shouldn't kiss her here, but I couldn't resist. My lips settled over hers, brushing back and forth until her lips parted. My tongue slid against hers, the honeyed melon flavor of her wine coated her mouth.

I stepped back. "I'm starving. Are you ready to leave?"

"Yes. I didn't eat much today. Let's go."

I slid an arm around her waist, keeping her close as I pushed open the exit door. I had taken a few steps when I noticed a man standing at the end of the alley. He wore a long black trench coat, even though it was an unseasonably warm night in May. I shoved Hattie behind me, cursing inwardly that I didn't bring my gun.

"What's wrong?" Hattie whispered, one hand clutching the back of my shirt and the other on top of my left shoulder.

"Go back inside."

"No. I'm not leaving you."

"Now!" I yelled, brushing her hand off my shoulder.

"Don't move. Either of you," the man said, flashing the gun strapped to his waist.

I pushed Hattie aside, and she stumbled, crying out as she fell on all fours. I ran forward, my feet pounding against the asphalt. When I closed the distance between us, I launched myself at the man, shoving him against the brick wall. The air whooshed out of his lungs, and his body sagged like a rag doll.

I wrapped my hands around his neck and smashed his head against the wall, each sickening thud acted like gasoline fueling my anger.

He sneered as his fist connected with the side of my face. My chin whipped to the side. Blood exploded from my lip and the taste of iron seeped into my mouth. The man lifted his gun, but I grabbed his wrist, slamming it against the wall until it fell out of his hand, clanging against the cracked asphalt.

He kicked my knee, and I grunted as pain radiated up my leg. Adrenaline flowed through my body, igniting a murderous fury. I dove forward, caging my arms around his waist, tackling him. Straddling him with my legs, I put him in a chokehold. The man bucked underneath me, clawing at my hands. Blood oozed over my fingertips like black lava from the back of the man's head. Gasping, his lips turned a faint shade of blue. Violence hemorrhaged from my pores. I wanted to kill him. I was going to kill him.

Distantly, Hattie's shrill screams vibrated down the manmade corridor of brick, stone, and cement, but I was too preoccupied with delivering violence to focus on her. Sweat dripped down my temples, mingling with the blood seeping from my lip. My Vargas bloodline craved death— the split second in time when the soul abandoned its physical form, and the eyes dimmed for eternity. The darkness inside me eclipsed the light.

My fist collided with his face.

Once.

Twice.

Three times.

I couldn't stop. I loosened the reins on the darkness living deep inside of my soul. I was blind and deaf to everything except the bloodlust crackling in my synapses.

A car screeched to halt at the end of the alley. A second man ran out of the car flashing his gun. The silver glittered, reflecting off the street lamp.

"Let him go," the man yelled, pointing his gun between my eyes.

I rolled back, lifting my hands into the air. "What do you want?"

The second man ignored me. "John, get the fuck up," he spat at the man moaning on the ground where I left him.

"We're here to deliver a message," the man with the gun said through clenched teeth, his body half turned away from me.

I glanced over my shoulder, searching for Hattie. She was crouched into a ball near the dumpster, tears streaming down her face.

I shot to my feet, angling my body to protect Hattie. I kicked the gun I wrestled from the first attacker behind me, but within my reach. "Then, deliver your fucking message and leave."

"Senator Deveron said the game is up. He knows who you are. You have twenty-four hours to do as he requested, or he'll expose you."

I glanced back at Hattie. Her mouth was parted as she stared wide-eyed at me, her entire body trembling. My chest heaving with exertion, I rolled my shoulders back. "Great. I have a message for him too."

The man with the gun shrugged, trying to look casual even as his eyes flickered between Hattie and me.

I scooped up the discarded gun and aimed. "Tell Senator Deveron to go to hell. Now get the fuck out of here before I kill you both."

I watched them get in the car and drive away. I wiped the blood from my mouth with the back of my hand and turned to face Hattie.

"Hattie," I said, kneeling in front of her. "Are you okay?"

"Ryker." She grabbed my hand, squeezing it, her eyes filling with fresh tears. "Please tell me what's going on. Why would Senator Deveron come after you? What does he want?"

My stomached clenched as I cradled her hand between both of mine. "I don't know."

She yanked her hand from mine. "Dammit, Ryker. I need to know. I'm running blind. How can I protect myself when I don't know what's going on?"

She was right. "You don't have to. That's my job."

"You can't shadow me for the rest of my life. Tell me the truth."

"No," I snapped.

She stood, brushing invisible debris from her sunflower-colored dress with one hand and clutching her purse with the other. "Then, I'm done."

"What do you mean?"

She scraped her hair away from her face, her fingers noticeably shaking. "Our relationship has run its course. We can't be together in public. You can't or won't tell me the truth. People are waving guns at me, trying to physically assault us. It's over." She started walking down the alley, her heels clicking like a time bomb with every step.

My chest caved. Everything in me screamed to let her go. That this wouldn't work. That we could never be anything. Rever was right. My relationship with Hattie would blow up in my face.

"Wait," I yelled when she reached the mouth of the alley. She glanced over her shoulder, her amber eyes glowing with hope. "Okay," I conceded.

"Okay, what?"

"I'll tell you the truth."

"Everything?"

I scrubbed my hands over my face. This was fucking nuts. Something was wrong with me, but knowing it didn't stop me. "Yes, everything I know."

Chapter Twelve

Hattie

Ryker opened the door to his apartment. I paused at the threshold. Once I knew the truth, my whole life would change. As much as I wanted to unravel all the lies, I was afraid.

His eyebrows lifted slightly…expectantly. "Are you coming in?"

I took a tentative step back. What was I doing? Did I really want to know the truth? Did I really want to alienate my friends and family for a man I didn't know? Could I trust him? My gaze darted down the hall in the direction of the elevator, and for a brief second, I considered running away from him. From everything. From everyone. I could move across the country and start over, become somebody different. Somebody better. Stronger.

"Hattie. What are you doing?"

An involuntary whimper escaped my mouth. I could've been killed tonight. Even though I'd left Mexico, nothing had changed. "I'm scared."

"I'm not going to let anyone hurt you," he said,

his voice soft, almost gentle.

His words should've reassured me, but they didn't. Instead, they made me realize I was in danger. He believed I was in danger.

I closed my eyes and shook my head. "You can't control everything."

The roughened pads of his fingers skated down my face, caressing my cheek. A tremor of desire and fear raced down my spine.

"You're right, but are you willing to give up so easily?"

I opened my eyes and lifted my chin. I wasn't a quitter. "No."

One side of his mouth curled up into a lopsided grin. "I didn't think so."

He threaded his fingers through mine, pulling me through his nearly empty apartment. I scanned the empty walls, the bare floors, and the smattering of furniture. "This is—"

He shrugged. "Not much of a home. I've never gotten around to doing anything."

I trailed my finger through the veil of dust on a small rectangular table, leaving a clean line on the espresso-colored wood. "How long have you lived here?"

"Five years."

My eyebrows jumped up my forehead. "Wow."

"I know." He chuckled. "Come with me. We can talk in my office."

We reached the end of the hall, and he pulled his keys out of his pocket, unlocking a dark-walnut paneled door.

"Why the secrecy?" I asked, stepping into the

room.

"I don't like anyone going through my papers. Sit." He motioned to a chair in front of his desk.

"So formal," I said. As I settled into the chair, a giggle escaped out of my mouth, more from nerves than the situation. The rich smell of worn leather enveloped me.

He pulled a file folder out of a desk drawer and settled into lounge chair behind the desk. "Did you tell Evan anything about us?"

"No. I haven't talked to him since that night at the restaurant." His eyes narrowed. "I know I promised to call him, but I haven't done it. I didn't know what to say to him."

He opened the file folder, but I couldn't see anything. "What about Vera?"

"Nothing. I swear. Except—"

"Except what?"

Blood flooded my cheeks. "I told her I was seeing someone, but I refused to tell her any details about you or us."

"You didn't tell anyone else? A therapist? Maybe you wrote something in a diary or a journal."

"No." Then, I remembered the pregnancy test I never removed from cabinet underneath the sink. My stomach dropped. "Well, I took a pregnancy test. I hid it under the bathroom sink at Evan's apartment. I didn't want to put it in the trash, but then I forgot about it."

Ryker leaned back in his chair. "He'd think it was his."

"No, he wouldn't. We haven't..." My voice

trailed off. I didn't want to have this conversation with him. "Just no."

"What I tell you right now cannot go anywhere. You can't tell your family. You can't tell Vera, and you certainly can't confront Evan or his family."

I nodded, and he slid a piece of paper across the desk. "What's this?"

"A wire transfer from Senator Deveron to me."

I scanned the paper. "Five hundred thousand dollars? What's this for?"

"Check the date?"

"March 1."

"What happened around then?"

I shifted closer, leaning my elbows on his desk as I shook my head, laboring to remember every detail. "Nothing." I cocked my head to the side. "I broke up with Evan right around that time, and you know what happened after that. I went to Mexico with Vera for Spring Break, then you…" My heart sputtered as pieces of the puzzle shifted in my mind.

Ryker stood up and walked around the corner of the desk, pausing in front of me with his hands shoved deep into his pockets. "Then I found you in that bar in Mexico."

The air exploded out of my lungs like I'd been kicked in the gut, and the room tilted. I clutched the edge of the desk, suffocating on the noxious fumes of betrayal. "Did…" I blinked, stalling for time.

Please don't be true.

With deadened hands, I rubbed my temples. "Did Senator Deveron pay you to abduct me?"

"Yes."

One simple word. By itself, it was innocuous,

innocent even, but it felt like he had pulled the safety pin on a grenade and fractured my life into a million pieces. I jumped out of the chair like a jack in the box.

"No," I yelled. "It's not true. He wouldn't do that. It doesn't make sense. Evan would never let him." Ryker shook his head, his face lined with pity. I felt sick. My hands shook. My heart pounded against my chest like a battering ram. Then, my knees buckled like a folding chair.

Ryker caught me, his fingers digging into my upper arms. "Breathe, Hattie. Breathe."

I didn't want to breathe. I didn't want to open my eyes. I wanted it all to go away. I wanted to disappear. Fade away. "Why? Tell me why, Ryker." I swallowed against the surge of nausea, contorting my stomach into a pretzel. God, I fucking hurt everywhere.

His hand moved up and down my back, and he kissed the top of my head. "They need you. They need your dad, but I think you already know this part. I told you all of this in Mexico, but I omitted the names of the parties involved."

Squeezing my eyes shut, I skimmed through the murky conversations with Ryker and Ignacio. Then, it hit me. According to Ignacio, Rever had offered information about politicians and businessmen affiliated with the Vargas Cartel in exchange for prosecutorial immunity. He needed leverage to stop it from happening. So did Senator Deveron. I tilted up my head, searching Ryker's face.

"Senator Deveron has connections to the Vargas Cartel." It wasn't a question. It was a statement, but the minute I said it, I realized it was the absolute truth. Deep down maybe I knew all along. Ignacio and Ryker had given me enough hints, but I refused to see the truth. The truth butchered me.

Ryker nodded. "It started fifteen years ago. Senator Deveron's Las Vegas casino was on the verge of bankruptcy. Ignacio propositioned him. Ignacio needed a way to launder drug money, and Senator Deveron needed a quick cash infusion. It made sense for both of them. When President Felipe Calderón took power in 2006, he declared war on the drug cartels. The Vargas Cartel experienced significant losses. Senator Deveron needed the Vargas Cartel's money to keep his casino afloat, but he also wanted more power and influence, so he ran for Senate. The Vargas Cartel funneled money to his campaign through dummy corporations, campaign bundlers, and non-profits with the understanding that he'd use his power to help the cartel."

"So you're saying Senator Deveron is a puppet of the Vargas Cartel."

"No, more like they have a symbiotic relationship. Senator Deveron uses his position to block the U.S. from interfering with the Vargas Cartel's trafficking activities, and he blocks active prosecution of the cartel's top officials."

"Oh my God," I whispered.

"The Vargas Cartel supplies ninety percent of the drugs that enter Nevada, and it has a significant presence in the western United States."

Dazed, I stepped out of his embrace and walked to the window, my back facing him. "I didn't realize that." I stared at the lights flickering in the inky sky. "I don't know why they need my dad or me. It sounds like Senator Deveron can take care of himself. He has all the power and connections he needs."

"Rever leaked some information implicating Senator Deveron, but reports of his connection to the Vargas Cartel have been bubbling up for the last two years. He needs a way to stop the inevitable."

His hands dropped on my shoulders, and part of me wanted to push him away. Push everyone away. I was utterly exhausted. My mind spun in circles as I struggled to unravel fiction and truth.

"What are you saying?"

"If you marry Evan, your dad would have a strong incentive to kill any investigation that landed on his desk."

A shiver trickled down my spine, and I felt cold...so fucking cold. Frost crawled through my body, numbing every cell in its path. I didn't think I'd ever be warm again. "Ah, I see." Avoiding Ryker's heated stare, I crossed the room and snagged my purse off the chair.

"What do you see?"

"Evan strung me along all this time for what I could offer his family. You abducted me for money, and then you wanted me to get back together with Evan last week for what reason? More money? To help the Vargas Cartel smuggle more drugs?"

"Hattie." He grabbed my hand, but I slapped it away. The sound of flesh hitting flesh echoed through the room.

"Don't touch me," I spat through clenched teeth.

"All week, I had this internal debate running in my head whether we could actually make this work between us. I twisted reality. I distorted the facts, and somehow I convinced myself if we wanted it enough, we'd figure it out. We could be together."

"We can."

I scoffed. "No, you're wrong. You were ready to let me go last week. Why should I believe you won't change your mind when a better offer comes along?" I sucked in a deep breath, willing the tears to disappear from the corner of my eyes. Willing my heart to freeze over and become an impenetrable wall of icy disdain. Willing myself to evolve from the pathetically gullible pawn I'd become into someone stronger. Smarter. Braver.

"Because I choose you. I choose you over the safety of my family and over everything I've worked for. I refused to help him. Why do you think he came after me today?" I shrugged. "I told him to leave you alone."

I blew my bangs out of my eyes. "Right. For now. For today."

"I'm not letting you go again. I'm done fighting what's happening between us. We're in this together. To the end. This bullshit with Senator Deveron and the Vargas Cartel will fade away, but what I feel for you won't. I realize that now."

"I have to go. This is too much," I said, taking a half step to the door, my head shaking back and forth, but I didn't want to leave. I never wanted to leave him. A few pretty words and my anger disintegrated like a sandcastle in a windstorm. How did he do that? From the moment I saw him in that bar I was a goner. My body chose him over and over, even when my mind begged me to hate him.

His head whipped toward mine, his eyes blistering with passion. "Senator Deveron threatened to withdraw the protection of the U.S. government from the Vargas Cartel and align with the Alvarez Cartel."

I rolled my eyes and leaned against the desk. "That doesn't make sense. The U.S. government doesn't protect or align with drug cartels."

One of his dark eyebrows lifted ever so slightly. "Don't be naïve. Of course they do. The U.S. government, through the ICE, ATF, and DEA, have a record of providing benefits and immunity to cartels—particularly the Vargas Cartel—in exchange for receiving information against other cartels. What do you think the 'Fast and Furious' gun-running program to Mexican cartels paid for by the U.S. taxpayers was about?"

I pinched the bridge of my nose. "I don't get it. Why would the U.S. government do that?"

His mouth twisted, and his hand sliced through the air. "Because everything is never as simple as it seems on the surface. Nothing is black and white, especially when it comes to the government. Some insiders think the CIA actually orchestrates the global narcotics trade and facilitates laundering the profits."

Tensing inwardly, I squeezed my purse until my knuckles whitened. "That's crazy."

Sighing, he said, "Maybe, maybe not, but do you realize what would happen to my family if the U.S. government threw its resources behind the Alvarez

Cartel?"

"The Vargas Cartel would make less money," I mocked.

Ryker slammed his open palm against the desk, frustration etched into every line of his face. "No. I wish that were all it meant. Wouldn't that be simple?"

I balled my hands into fists. "Then what?"

Ryker raked his hands through his already disheveled hair, bringing attention to his bloodied and cracked knuckles. "The U.S. government would supply a steady stream of AK-47s to the Alvarez Cartel, along with other small favors that would give them the advantage. They'd finally have the manpower and weapons to overpower the Vargas Cartel."

"Ignacio will figure it out. He's a survivor. He said as much to me many times," I spat, packing as much disdain as possible into my words.

"No, he won't. He won't last three months," he countered, his voice harsh.

"What do you mean?" I asked, struggling to make my face as expressionless as possible.

"He'll be killed, or the U.S. Government would indict him on drug trafficking charges along with a hundred other things."

Remorse trickled through my veins, but I clamped down on the emotion before it took root. Even though I didn't like Ignacio, I didn't want Ryker to suffer. "You really believe that would happen?"

Ryker exhaled loudly, deep lines bracketing his mouth. "I know it would. Senator Deveron told me as much. The minute he rips the veil from the Vargas Cartel, it's over."

"So what are you going to do?"

"I'm not going to hand you over to Evan or Senator Deveron, if that's what you're asking. I tried, but I'm too selfish to give you up." His voice was simultaneously soft and rough, like the syrupy nectar dripping from the prickly blue agave plant.

Relief coursed through me. "You're not?"

"No." He grabbed my hand, threading his fingers through mine, and this time I didn't resist. "I told you. I choose you. I want you. We're going to make this work."

I chewed on my lower lip. "Then what's going to happen?"

"If he follows through with his threats, I'll take him down."

"How would you do that?"

He shrugged, but his metallic eyes glittered with anger. "I'll expose him."

"Does he know that?"

Ryker rubbed the back of his neck, and the muscles in his jaw constricted. "He knows. I told him."

I gazed at him for a few agonizing beats, processing the implications of his words while my heart splintered. I hooked my arms around his neck to steady my anxiety as a puzzled frown creased my forehead. "Won't that mean exposing you and your family too?"

He hauled me against his chest, eliminating any space between our bodies, and a frisson of desire zipped through my nerve endings. "It might, but I'm more concerned with keeping you safe. I'll figure out the rest as we go."

I nodded, inhaling his scent, absorbing his nearness. Being around him, touching him, made me feel safe again. I wanted to forget about all the dirty details he confessed and trust Ryker to make everything right. He said he'd take care of it, and he hadn't let me down yet. Blindly believing him might make me naïve, but I didn't want to worry about it right then. "What now?" I whispered as I pressed soft kisses against the thick column of his neck.

"I want to take a shower, and then I believe I owe you dinner." His face radiated intensity, desire, and something primal. Suddenly, the air crackled with lust instead of anger and betrayal.

With a tremulous smile, I brushed the pads of my fingers over the cut on his lower lip. "Okay."

Chapter Thirteen

Ryker

Without second-guessing myself, I guided Hattie into the bathroom with me, my hand pressed into the small of her back. All week I wanted to move beyond a few heated kisses, but I'd been waiting. For what? I didn't know. The right moment. With the way things were going, I didn't think it'd ever happen, but it was virtually impossible for me to walk away from her and never look back. She had chiseled her way into my heart, infecting me with her smile, long legs, and her golden, cat-like eyes.

I closed the bathroom door behind us and turned on the shower. She leaned against the bathroom counter as I scrubbed the blood from my hands. Steam filled the bathroom, fogging the mirrors and sheltering us from the outside world.

I unbuttoned my shirt and tossed it on the floor. My shoes, socks, pants, and boxer briefs followed. She still hadn't moved, but her eyes tracked my movements beneath the fringe of her lashes. With her lips pursed into a straight line and two deep grooves between her brows, she looked conflicted, as if she didn't know if she wanted to stay or go. She didn't need to worry. She was definitely staying. I'd already decided. She just didn't know it yet. I needed to claim her again, remind her she was mine. But more than anything, I needed to be inside of her again. It'd been too long.

Not allowing her to fight the magnetic pull between us, I trapped her against the bathroom counter with my hips and framed her face with my hands. Suspended in the moment, steam billowed around us as my lips hovered just inches from hers, and then I pulled her toward me. When my lips crashed against hers, a muffled moan escaped her lips, throwing fuel on the lust I barely held in check over the past week. Damn, I missed her. I had tried to close the box on our time together, compartmentalizing it and burying it, but it never disappeared. It never faded.

My tongue curled around hers, rough and demanding, taking her, showing her she was mine. I didn't hold anything back. The fruity taste of her wine lingered in her mouth. Her breathing accelerated in time with mine, and my stomach tightened with desire. By some sick twist of fate, we were meant to be together, and I intended to take advantage it.

I unzipped the back her dress as I kissed the smooth skin of her neck and her collarbone, savoring her, consuming her, and biting her. Her yellow shift dress pooled at her feet and my breath splintered. She looked even more beautiful than I remembered.

Golden skin.

Long toned legs.

Perfectly molded curves.

The seductive upward tilt of her lips.

Right then, I realized she owned me long before we exchanged a single word in that bar in Mexico. Now, the damage was complete. I was hooked. Addicted. Obsessed. Strung out for her, and I couldn't force myself to regret it.

Not wasting a single second, I reached around the curve of her waist and unhooked her bra. I bit back a groan as the black lace slid off her body, exposing her pebbled nipples. I slipped her matching panties down her legs, trailing my fingers along the contours of her legs. Goosebumps tumbled like dominos down her arms and legs. And fuck if that didn't make me twice as hard as I was thirty seconds earlier.

Gathering her close, I pressed my lips against hers again as I blindly guided her to the shower. We bumped into the hamper, the shower door, and I nearly tripped over the shower curb, but none of it mattered as the hot water poured over our bodies and the steam clouded our already lust muddled vision. This moment was about us. Not Senator Deveron. Not Evan. Not the Vargas Cartel. Just us.

I moved my palms along the soft angles of her body, tracing every curve, swell, and dip. I couldn't get enough of her.

Breasts.

Waist.

Hips.

Navel.

The curve of her backside.

All of it perfect. Perfect for me.

And then I cupped her mound, rubbing her, caressing her, teasing her everywhere but where we both wanted me to go. She rocked against my hand as whimpers and disjointed pleas spilled like water from her mouth.

"Shh," I said, touching my fingertips to her lips. Her breath was jagged, heated, and electric against my skin. "I'll take care of you."

I slid one finger inside of her, then two, gliding my fingers back and forth. Her head tipped up, arching her body forward, like a pagan offering. The Roman goddess, Venus, in the flesh. I pulled her nipple in my mouth, sucking her until a fractured gasp fell from her parted lips. Like someone struck a match, my insides lit on fire.

"More," she whispered. I moved to the other nipple, sucking, biting, and giving it equal attention. Equal love. Her entire body tensed, vibrating with desire. She was close. So fucking close, and I didn't want her to go over the edge yet. I needed to explore and taste every inch of her, bringing her to the brink over and over until she couldn't imagine life without me. I pulled my fingers from her wet heat.

"No," she murmured, her eyes popping open, glazed, dilated, and a little confused. She was adorable and she was mine. Nothing would separate us again. I didn't care what I had to do to keep her. I'd do it without a second thought. I was done playing games. I was done fixing the problems of the greed-corrupted, power-obsessed one percent of the population. I wanted to live my life, and that life would include Hattie.

Even without Hattie in my life, my career as a fixer had come to an end. My cover was blown. My confrontation with Senator Deveron's men illustrated that fact loud and clear. It wouldn't be long before the rest of the world connected the dots between Ry Fallon the campaign bundler and Ryker Vargas the fixer.

I lifted one of her knees, propping it on the marble shower bench. Her hands clamped around my shoulders, digging into my skin. I kneeled in front of her, and her hands knotted in the wet strands of my hair.

My eyes never left hers as my hands slid up her thighs. A red tinge colored her cheeks. I flicked my tongue along her opening, tasting her, worshipping her, and devouring her honeyed pleasure until her sighs and moans echoed like a sonata off the marbled walls. She was flushed and shaking, and I was harder than I ever remembered as she cried out her release. Her knees buckled. I steadied her with my hands as I kissed her hipbone, her navel, skimming my mouth up her torso, reacquainting myself with every detail of her body. I wrapped her legs around my waist and turned off the shower.

She buried her head in the crook of my neck. "Where are we going?"

"To bed."

"Mm," she hummed. The simple sound vibrated like an electrical current through my body.

Without turning on the bedroom light, I placed her on my bed and grabbed a condom from the nightstand. As I rolled it on, I watched the way the moonlight from the window danced over her skin. Being with this woman did crazy things to me.

I crawled onto the bed and guided her onto her back. I spread her legs one at a time, positioning her so she was open and waiting for me. I traced the lines of her face with my fingers, committing every angle to memory. My mouth closed over hers, taking pleasure in the sweet taste of her mouth. Our hips rocked together, and my cock slid back and forth against her entrance. Each pass along her sex extracted a needy whimper from her parted lips. One flex of my hips and I could be buried deep inside of her, but I held back.

"Please," she whispered as her fingernails dug into my back, trying to guide me inside of her.

My tip penetrated her sex an inch, and I gritted my teeth to stop myself from thrusting into her. I wanted to draw out every second of this reunion. I never wanted it to end.

"I'm dying here. It's been so long," she pleaded as I pulled out again.

"I know," I growled, slowly moving inside of her again, just halfway. Her walls twitched around me, and I bit the inside of my cheek.

"Ohh." Her hands clawed at the sheets, and her hips lurched off the bed in invitation. "That's perfect. Keep going."

Satisfaction rushed through my veins. Sweat beaded my brow, and I couldn't hold back any longer. I couldn't deny her or myself for one more second. I slammed into her, giving her everything I had. Taking more than my share. A long groan burst from my mouth.

Without much effort, our hips synchronized like we'd done this hundreds of times. God knows, I had replayed every moment I was inside of her at least a hundred times over the past month.

I sucked on the top of her collarbone, branding her as mine. The thought fueled my need for her. I gripped her hips as I pounded into her. She circled her legs around my waist, pulling me deeper and deeper, meeting me thrust for thrust until we were two halves of a whole.

The bed frame squeaked. The headboard crashed with methodical repetition against the wall. Vaguely, I remembered Rever in the guest bedroom adjacent to mine, and the open blinds. I couldn't bring myself to care about any of it. The way her walls contracted around me and the tension building at the base of my spine with every mindless thrust demanded every ounce of my attention and more.

And then Hattie exploded, her scream the crescendo to our symphony of moans and groans. She tightened around me, and I teetered on the edge seesawing back of forth, trying to maintain my rhythm, trying to keep going, trying to keep thrusting. But it was too hard. She felt too good. Sparks shot through my body. Her name tumbled from my lips, sounding more like a howl than a word, and I couldn't stop the pleasure induced insanity as it ripped through my body, hurling me into oblivion.

I stopped moving and opened my eyes. She was staring at me. She looked soft and dreamy.

"Hi," she whispered as her fingers traced my

jaw.

"Hi," I whispered back, at a loss for words because everything felt too perfect to describe. The vulnerability of the moment rattled my heart and tore at my gut, but I wouldn't take it back for anything. She was in my blood, and I was ready to accept it, regardless of what happened. Good or bad.

I kissed her, explaining without words what she meant to me and how I'd never let her go.

I rolled off her and gathered her into my arms. "Promise me something."

Hattie turned her head to the side, a faint smile on her face. "What?"

"Don't confront Evan or say anything to your family. Let me take care of it."

"I can't do that."

"Hattie, give yourself a few days to process this, and then if you still want to confront him, I'll go with you."

She nodded, propping her body up on her elbow. "When are we going to eat? I'm starving."

I laughed. "Now."

Chapter Fourteen

Hattie

Fog blanketed the city this morning, coating the pink blooms of the cherry blossoms in a blurry haze, making them less vibrant. Less alive. The temperature had dropped in the short walk from Ryker's apartment to Evan's townhome. A gust of wind, thick with grime and the smell of moisture, whipped through my hair.

This morning, I woke up in a daze, numbed by everything Ryker told me about Evan and his father last night. Even Ryker's smiles and reassuring words didn't improve my mood.

Like someone had kicked me in the gut, betrayal simmered in my stomach, making me simultaneously angry and nauseous. I had to do something to reclaim my life, so a half hour after Ryker left me alone in his bed, I found myself standing in front of the door to Evan's townhouse.

Drawing in a lungful of heavy, moisture-laden air, I fortified my wilting willpower to do what I had to do. In order to understand everything, I needed more information from as many sources as possible. A chilly gust of wind whistled through the trees and I shivered, wishing I'd worn a heavier jacket.

My heart racing violently, I glanced left, then right. Looking for what?

Evan.

Senator Deveron.

My mom.

Ryker.

I didn't know. When I didn't recognize anyone on the street, I pulled my keys out of my pocket. Evan never asked me to return the key to his place, and I hadn't thought about it until this morning when I started planning my next move.

Ryker had warned me not to confront Evan, and I promised I wouldn't, but I lied. I'd had enough. I counted the minutes until Ryker left this morning, not because I didn't want to spend time with him, but because I intended to go back to the townhome I used to share with Evan.

The alarm beeped repeatedly when I pushed the door open. Thank God, he wasn't home. I entered the code and dropped my purse on the kitchen counter. I glanced around the room. Everything looked the same, but dirtier. An abandoned cereal bowl and coffee cup sat on the countertop. Books were stacked haphazardly on the coffee table on top of a closed pizza box.

I slipped my phone out of my pocket and texted Evan.

Me: Where are you?

He replied almost immediately.

Evan: *Office hours. I'll be here for another twenty minutes. Why?*

Perfect. I wanted to search the apartment before he came home.

Me: *At your place. I want to talk.*

Evan: *Okay. I'll be home in thirty minutes.*

I tossed my phone on the counter.

I didn't waste a second. I darted into the bedroom. The room looked partially abandoned. Nails littered the wall where I had hung pictures of Evan and me. He had stripped the bedding from the mattress. It didn't look like he'd moved back into the bedroom after I left. I shrugged, pushing away any emotions. I couldn't worry about Evan anymore. He sure as hell didn't care about me.

I flung open the closet doors. I had left some clothes in the bedroom closet, not because I thought I'd be back, but because I didn't have much room at Vera's apartment. I stripped off the dress I wore last night and changed into some old jeans and a blouse. I stuffed my dress and a few other clothes into my purse.

After I had finished dressing, I ran into the guest bedroom. Evan used it as his personal study. I flung open every drawer. I didn't know what I thought I'd find. After all, as of two weeks ago, I shared this study with Evan, but I couldn't search Senator

Deveron's private files.

Keys.

An empty notepad.

Receipts.

Bills.

Nothing. I propped my elbows on top of the desk, thinking where Evan would keep incriminating evidence. As my eyes scanned the room, I spotted the black leather case of his iPad.

I stared at the keypad, searching the recesses of my memory for clues to Evan's passcode. I recalled a conversation when he revealed he used birthdays for all of his passcodes. I tried his birthday. My birthday. Then, I tried a combination of our birthdays—eleven and fifteen. It worked. Icons filled the screen.

I scanned through his email looking for anything referencing me. Then, I searched through his folders. One named HWC caught my attention. My initials? Hattie Waverly Covington? Maybe he organized all our correspondence into one folder.

I carried the iPad into the kitchen so Evan wouldn't surprise me when he came home. Sitting on a chair facing the front door, I touched the screen, opening the HWC folder. As I scrolled down the page, I saw at least fifty emails with subject lines referencing me, but none of them were from me.

I clicked on one from a few days ago.

To: EDeveron11
From: LV22
Evan,
Attached please find a few photos

documenting the subject's moves over the last few weeks. Let me know if you'd like to install listening devices at her current residence as well. We have permission to proceed.
Luke Viper
Viper Investigations

My hand shaking, I clicked on the first attachment. It was a picture of Ryker and me at the park. The second attachment was a picture of Ryker and me walking out of the back entrance of the bar a few blocks from his home.

My stomach twisted as I clicked through three other pictures. All of them were of me. Running. Eating. Leaving Vera's apartment. Every picture included a date stamp in the lower right-hand corner.

I searched for more emails from Viper Investigations. There were at least ten dating from before I left for Mexico. They contained more pictures, detailed schedules outlining how I spent my day. There was no doubt about it—Evan had someone following me and reporting all my moves back to him since we broke up the first time.

When Ryker implicated Evan and his father in my abduction, part of me held out hope Evan wasn't involved. That he was his father's pawn in this whole scheme. But as I clicked on picture after picture and email after email, it became painfully obvious Evan actively participated in my abduction.

I checked the clock. Evan would be home in less than ten minutes. I scrolled through his inbox, clicking on random emails. Most of them were more of the same. Then, my heart nearly seized in my chest when I spotted an email from Vera. I squeezed my eyes as my finger hovered over the iPad. A chill darted down my spine. I sucked in a deep breath, and then I clicked on the email.

To: EDeveron11
From: VeraWatts
Evan,
Hattie hasn't told me anything. Stop texting me. Stop emailing me. Stop calling me. I can't help you and even if I could, I wouldn't. I sent you those pictures from Mexico, but it was wrong. You're on your own.
Vera

As I sat there in the silence of Evan's townhouse, I realized I didn't know anything. Without a doubt, I had spent the last few years of my life in the dark, blind to everything and everyone. Every single moment of my life had been a carefully crafted illusion. All the lies I had yet to discover scared the shit out of me. How far back did the deception go? Was anything with Evan ever real? Horror-struck at myself for caring, I flipped the iPad over so I wouldn't be tempted to read anything else. I had read enough. I had seen enough…for now.

My hands curled into fists as I stared at the door, waiting for Evan to open it. With every passing second, anger curled through my body, tainting me with a venomous fury, and robbing me of rational thought. Diabolical plots for revenge flickered unbidden through my mind. Rage sharpened my thoughts and calibrated my vision. I embraced it. I reveled in it. I got drunk on it.

Evan and his dad wanted to play games with my life. Well, turnabout was fair play. I'd spent too much time embracing my martyrdom like I was next in line to be canonized and declared a saint. Fuck that. I wasn't a saint, and I refused to be a martyr. I slipped the gun I found in Ryker's closet from my purse and leaned back in the chair, waiting for him to open the door.

I didn't have to wait long. Evan walked in the door five minutes later.

"Hattie, I'm glad you stopped by," Evan said as he strolled into his home with a big smile on his face. "I was going to call you—" Evan froze mid-sentence, eyeing the gun on the table in front of me. "Why do you have a gun?"

I ran the pads of my fingers over the barrel of the gun, locking eyes with my deranged ex-fiancé. Before today, I didn't believe it was possible to hate someone as much as I hated Evan and his slimy dad. "I thought I'd bring some protection."

Evan's eyebrows slanted downward. "What the hell are you talking about? I would never hurt you."

I raised one eyebrow and smirked. "Really? Your actions prove otherwise."

Evan lifted his hands up in mock surrender as he shook his head. "I don't know what you're talking about, but you're scaring me. Have you been skipping your therapy sessions?"

Clenching my teeth, I trembled with pent-up aggression. The amount of hatred and anger seeping out of my pores could've slayed an army. I flipped over his iPad, slamming it against the counter. Pounding my index finger against the screen, I typed in his passcode. "While you were out, I took the liberty of scanning through an email folder labeled HWC. Does that change your perspective?"

Evan stuffed his hands into his pockets and licked his lower lip as his eyes looked everywhere but at me. Fucking shifty-eyed bastard. "It's not what you think," he mumbled.

I folded my arms across my chest. "So you're not having me followed?"

His shoulders sagged. "I am, but only because I don't want something to happen to you again. Even though we're not together anymore, I haven't stopped caring about you, loving you. I was crazed when you were abducted. I couldn't sleep. I barely ate. I didn't go to class. I can't go through that again."

"All signs of a guilty conscience."

He repeatedly swallowed, his Adam's apple rocking up and down like a fishing bobber. "You're right. I felt guilty because you should have been in the Virgin Islands with me. I made a bad decision that hurt you. All of this could've been avoided if I had been faithful."

Laughing, I stood up and walked around the table. "Sure, if I hadn't gone to that bar and caught you cheating on me, things may have been different, but then I would still be in the dark. I wouldn't know the extent of you and your dad's corruption."

"That's not true."

The stubborn set of Evan's jaw caused a flashflood of resentment to roar through me. What a liar. I lifted the gun and aimed it at the center of his chest. "Don't lie."

He took a step back, his eyes flickering back and forth between the gun and my face. "This is crazy. What are you doing? You don't need that." His voice cracked on the last word.

"I know your fucked up family arranged my abduction. Your dad planned everything, and you agreed because you're a spineless piece of shit—a puppet dancing to your dad's corrupt tune."

He sucked in a breath as a flash of surprise washed over his face. "We didn't—"

I shoved the muzzle of the gun against his chest, twisting it slowly from side to side. A sick and perverted satisfaction slid down my spine when I spotted the sweat beading his brow. "Shut the fuck up. It's too late. I know everything. I know you offered me up as a pawn to stop Rever Vargas from talking about your dad's criminal connections. I know you only wanted to marry me so my dad would have a reason to conceal your dad's connection to the Vargas Cartel."

"I didn't care about that. That's my dad's business. I did it for us. I love you, and I knew you wouldn't give me another chance. I didn't have any choice."

"Are you delusional? Are you seriously trying to argue you handed me over to a drug cartel because you loved me and wanted me back?"

A muscle twitched in his cheek. "They weren't supposed to hurt you. I wouldn't have agreed otherwise."

"Not hurt me?" Acid swirled in my gut. "And

you think that justifies what you did?"

"It was all a ruse to put pressure on your father and force the government to fast track Rever Vargas' release. That's why Ryker Vargas was involved. It was his job to shield you from the ugly side of the Cartel. He promised to keep you safe. You weren't supposed see anything except the inside of a room and take an occasional walk under heavy guard."

"Safe? A ruse?" I scoffed as my mind marinated in resentment. "Do you have any clue what actually happened to me?"

"No. You haven't told me anything," he accused. "Not one fucking thing. I've tried to get you to open up to me, but you've shot me down every single time. I wanted to help you move past it."

"They drugged me. They locked me in a room without windows until I didn't know if it was day or night. That maniac sliced my neck, but you already know that. We were attacked by a rival cartel, and I fucking killed a man."

He reached for my hand, shaking his head. "Hattie, I had no idea."

I lifted the gun and waved it in front of me. "I shot him. Blood splattered all over the trees, and I stared into his dead eyes. I'm a murderer."

"I'm sorry. I'm so sorry," he whispered. "You're not a murderer. It was self-defense. Nobody could claim otherwise."

I shrugged. "A technicality."

He rubbed his hand back and forth over his lips. "I never wanted to hurt you. You make me sound like an asshole."

"You did that all by yourself."

"Dammit, Hattie. If I had any idea what would happen, I wouldn't have agreed."

"Then you're a fucking idiot. What did you expect when you used me as collateral in your father's sick cover-up ploy?"

"That I'd find a way to make you love me again. That you'd see how much I love you and give me another chance. That you'd realize I'd always be there for you."

"Yeah, and how did that work out for you?" I snarled through clenched teeth. Every word out of my mouth fed my anger. I felt like a wild animal about to sink my teeth into my prey.

He bowed his head. "Not as expected, but maybe with more time—"

"No," I screamed. My hand itched to pull the trigger. Crazed thoughts rolled through my mind one after another. I was a lunatic and Evan was delusional. "Never. We're done. The next time you fuck with my life, I'll kill you. I won't even hesitate."

He closed his hand over the barrel of the gun, and I jerked it away. Our eyes locked. Did he ever love me or care about me? Why couldn't he understand how his selfishness nearly destroyed me? He said he didn't mean to hurt me, but I didn't believe him. I gawked at him, momentarily fooling myself into thinking if I looked hard enough, I'd be able to unravel his convoluted thoughts, or make sense of the madness, but I didn't see anything.

"Let me earn your trust again," he whispered, eyeing me carefully.

Bitterness whipped through my body. "I don't trust you. I'll never trust you. You don't understand the difference between the truth and a lie. You're a pathological liar and the son of a pathological liar. There's no hope for you."

"And you trust him?" he sneered.

"Who?"

He paused for a fraction, shifting his weight to his heels as he contemplated his answer. "Ryker Vargas."

I gnawed on the inside of my cheek. "It's none of your business. My life doesn't concern you."

"I don't know what he did to you, Hattie, but you can't trust him. I regret inviting that sick fuck into our life. He changed you. You're not the same anymore."

I dropped my hand to my side, and the gun brushed against my leg. "No shit," I mocked. "Imagine that. My boyfriend arranges to have me abducted by a drug cartel, and he questions why I'm not the same naïve person when I return home."

"He'll destroy you."

"He's not going to hurt me." I dropped my voice to a whisper, questioning the sanity of my words. "I trust him to keep me safe."

"Safe?" His eyebrows scaled his forehead as he moved his head from side to side. "What do you really know about Ryker Vargas?"

I tipped up my chin and smirked. "A lot more than you do, and he wouldn't lie to me, unlike you and your father."

"Are you serious?" he countered, his voice dark, dripping with venom. "We've known each for a long time. You're a smart girl. Think about what you're saying. He's the son of a drug lord. He has multiple identities. Do you know how he makes most of his money?"

"As a campaign bundler," I answered with a smile, trying to cover the thread of unease in my voice.

He snorted. "No. That's just his little side hobby to mask his real identity. He's a political fixer."

"A fixer," I echoed. "What's that supposed to mean?"

"He's a backroom operator who cleans up inconvenient messes for the privileged people who can afford his services."

"What kind of messes?"

Evan smirked, his brown eyes inky and narrowed in malice. "Dead bodies that need to disappear. Money transfers between criminal organizations and politicians. Bribing judges. Bribing lawmakers. All jobs a lawyer can't handle without stepping over the line."

Pain boomeranged through my body, and my upper eyelid twitched. "I don't believe you."

"How do you think my father found him? Why do you think he facilitated your abduction?"

"I don't care," I answered, stepping around him and walking to the door. I needed to get away from Evan and clear my head. "Just stay out my life. We're done."

My words didn't come out as forceful as I had wanted, but I couldn't find the energy to care. In the last few minutes, the anger had drained from my body. Undoubtedly, some amazing closing comments would float through my mind in a few hours, but at that instant, the right words eluded me.

"Wait," he called after me. "I found a pregnancy test hidden in the bathroom cabinet."

"So what?" I clutched the cold metal door handle in a death grip to steady my shaking hands. I had wondered if he found it, and I just got my answer.

"Are you pregnant?"

My shoulders sagged. Another blow and my battle-weary heart would shatter like glass. "Wouldn't you like to know?"

He moved closer to me, his footsteps a faint shuffle against the dark hardwood floors. "It wouldn't matter to me. We'd figure it out. If that's why you're with him, you don't have to—"

"No need to fall on your sword, Evan. Like I said, I don't want anything from you, except for you to leave me alone." I slammed the door behind me without looking back, enjoying the jarring finality of the sound. I wished I could believe this conversation would be the end of Senator Deveron and Evan's meddling in my life, but I wasn't a wide-eyed, gullible woman who believed in fairy tales, unicorns, and the pot of gold at the end of the rainbow. Not anymore.

A toxic mixture of melancholy and fury wrapped like thorns around my chest, twisting and twisting until I couldn't breathe. I had always known there was more to Ryker than his front as a campaign bundler. He was intimately familiar with the inner workings of the Vargas Cartel. He knew how to use a gun. He knew how to fight dirty. Part of me hoped if I ignored reality, it'd go away. We could ride off into the sunset and pretend none of it existed. A big happily ever after, but I guess people didn't get those in real life. Real life was full of half-truths, disappointments, and out-and-out lies.

Chapter Fifteen

Ryker

I was so sick of this shit. This was it. My last job. When my business cell rang at six o'clock in the morning, I didn't want to answer it. I wanted to stay with Hattie. Fortunately for my asshole client, I never quit in the middle of a job before, and I refused to start now. It'd leave the possibility of another enemy, and God knows, after the fallout with Senator Deveron, I had one more enemy than I needed already.

I parked my car one block from the gym where Representative Houser exercised from six to seven thirty every weekday. His routine never varied, which benefited people like me. I always cautioned my clients against being too predictable. It gave bad actors openings to take advantage of you.

I grabbed the black baseball cap from the passenger seat and put it on, pulling the brim down low enough to disguise my features on any cameras. I walked around to the side of the building where Representative Houser exited the building. I didn't understand why he didn't use the front door, but I refused to question my luck.

Representative Houser opened the door, his head down staring at his phone. What a jackass. For someone over his head in backroom deals, he should pay more attention to his surroundings. Backroom deals had a way of going bad quickly, at least in my experience.

Before he turned the corner to the parking lot behind the building, I wrapped my arm around his neck from behind him, eliminating the possibility he'd get a good look at my face.

"What the hell?" he yelled, scratching my arm.

"Shut the hell up and listen." I removed my gun from the holster under my coat and pressed it into the side of his head with my free arm.

"What do you want? My wallet is in my back pocket. Take it and leave me alone. I won't call the police."

"I don't want your fucking wallet."

He elbowed me in the side, and I rammed him face first into the brick wall. "Try that again, asshole, and you'll have a lot of explaining to do when you show up at work tomorrow with a black and blue face." I was tempted to do exactly as I threatened. He wouldn't be the first member of Congress to make up a story to explain getting the shit beat out of him as a result of his double-dealing.

"Don't do it. Don't hurt me," he said, sniffling like a fucking baby. "Just tell me what you want."

A dark, bitter laugh escaped my mouth. "I'm definitely going to leave you with a few bruises, but if you cooperate, all of them won't be on your face."

"I'll cooperate."

"Then, why are you planning to vote for the cyber security bill tomorrow?"

He groaned. "Tell them I'm sorry, but I changed my mind. I can't help your client. I'm getting too much pressure."

I grinded my gun against the back of his head and tightened my arm around his throat. "It doesn't work that way. You took their money."

"I can't do it." He shook his head. "I'm getting squeezed from both sides and I need to go with my conscience."

"You don't have a conscience." I banged his head against the wall again. Blood splattered on my shirt, and the metallic odor flooded my senses. Fucking hell. I'd have to burn this shirt. "You solicited and accepted bribes from both sides."

"I didn't," he protested, spitting a mixture of saliva and blood near my feet. *Asshole.* "I would never do that."

I punched him in the kidney. He'd be lucky if he weren't pissing blood tonight. "Don't lie."

"I'm not. I promise. I changed my mind. It's as simple as that." He repeatedly nodded, as if his word meant something. It didn't. He had his head shoved so far up the asshole of corruption, he couldn't see the truth if it kissed him on his shit-stained lips.

"So the hundred fifty thousand dollars that mysteriously landed in your Cayman Islands account five days ago was just a coincidence?"

"How do you know about that?"

"You accepted a bribe to kill this bill from one of the top cyber security firms that also happens to have one of the most infamous hackers on its payroll. Figure it out, dumbass. A few clicks of his more than capable fingers and he uncovered everything. It took him less than thirty minutes."

He craned he head to look at me, but I crammed his face into the wall.

"Don't turn around," I growled. "Keep your eyes glued to the wall and you'll be just fine."

"Okay, okay," he whispered. "What am I supposed to do? Either way I vote, I'm fucked. You'll kill me, and I don't want them as an enemy either."

"Oh, I won't kill you." I lived in the shadows, but I wasn't a murderer. I only killed in self-defense.

"You won't?" he said, his body drooping with relief. What a pansy.

"No. I have something far worse planned."

Tremors wracked his body, but I didn't have any compassion for him. He tried to play both sides. One bribe wasn't sufficient. Greedy bastard. "Return their money. Unwind the deal."

"I can't. I spent the money."

"I know you did. I know all about your gambling habit."

"You do?" he mumbled.

"Yes. I know you have a nice pay to play scheme going. I know you finance a half a million dollar a year gambling addiction by accepting bribes from anyone and everyone. You've been bought and sold so many times, you're worse than a dollar hooker."

"Only if their interests align with my beliefs."

"Your capacity for self-denial is almost as pathetic as your inability to control your addiction. What would your constituents think if they found out that while you preached about the need for more laws to stop the erosion of social norms and morals, you couldn't stop yourself from placing bet after bet all funded in some roundabout way by the American taxpayer?"

"I tried to stop," he mumbled, snot dripping down his face. It turned my stomach.

"I don't give a rat's ass what you tried to do. Save it for the media when I expose you for the piece of shit you are."

"No. No. I'll find a way to unwind the bribe. I'll come up with the money, and I'll vote against that bill."

I stood behind him as the seconds ticked by, letting him wonder if I believed him. If I'd allow him to go.

"Fine," I finally said. "But if you double-cross my client again, or if I even hear a single whisper you plan to vote for that bill, all of your dirty secrets will be on the front page of every major newspaper and website in excruciating detail, and not just your habit of taking bribes to fund your gambling addiction."

"I don't have any other secrets."

"You do…lots of them, and I have the pictures to prove it." I dropped my arm from his neck and slipped my gun into the holster around my waist. I pulled a rope out of my pocket, looped it around one of his wrists and tied the other end to the dumpster. "Wait here ten minutes and then you can leave."

When I was back in my car, I dialed the number of my contact at the cyber security firm.

"It's done."

"Good. The second half of your money will be wired to your account when the bill dies on the House floor tomorrow."

"Perfect."

"We have another job for you. It's in your inbox."

"No thanks. As of tonight, I'm out of business."

The man chuckled. "You're retiring? We both know that won't happen."

Hattie's golden eyes flashed through my mind. I couldn't live this type of life and have Hattie too. Even though we had an unconventional start, I wanted to make this work. "No. This time I'm out."

"Okay, you know how to find me if you change your mind."

I disconnected the phone call without responding. I had no intention of changing my mind.

Twenty minutes later, I opened the door to my apartment. Rever sat on the couch, his eyes glued to the television while he stuffed his face with pizza.

"I guess Hattie's not here."

"Nope," he answered without turning his head.

"When'd she leave?"

"Less than five minutes after you."

"Did she leave a note?"

Rever picked up a bottle of beer and took a long

pull. What happened to his vow to stop drinking? I guess it lasted as long as his bullshit about us being a family. Typical Rever. He'd never change. He only said and did things if they benefited him. He had the emotional depth of a puddle. At least I had my mom to give me a semblance of a real family. From what I knew of Rever's mom, she lived a separate life, pretending the ugliness of Ignacio's world and her son didn't exist. I almost felt sorry for Anna Alvarez. Then again, between Rever and whoever Juan Alvarez had lined up to marry her, Rever was probably the better choice.

"I didn't see one, but then, I don't really give a shit about her."

"What's wrong with you?"

Rever set his empty beer bottle on the coffee table. "Lots of things."

"Care to elaborate?"

Rever stood up and folded his arms across his chest. "I'd love to."

"Then get on with it," I said unenthusiastically, preparing myself for another one of Rever's tantrums.

With his hand on his hips, he paced back and forth. "Anna's still stuck in Mexico. We haven't made any plans to rescue her. I've been holed up in this apartment for weeks."

"Your doing, not mine," I interrupted.

"Whatever." Rever's hands sliced through the air. "But do you know the most fucked up part of what's happening right now?"

I rocked back on my heels as I glanced at my phone. I didn't have time to listen to Rever's dramatics tonight. I needed to find Hattie. I didn't want her living at Vera's house. She wasn't safe there until I wrapped up this mess with Senator Deveron. "No, but I have a feeling you're about to tell me."

"You're fucking up your life, and you're going to take the Vargas Cartel and me down with you."

My head snapped up. "What the hell are you talking about, and since when do you give a shit about the Vargas Cartel? You were ready to sell Ignacio down the river a month ago."

"I'm talking about Hattie fucking Covington."

I recoiled and my lips curled up, baring my teeth. "She's none of your business."

"She's my business now that Senator Deveron is crawling up your ass because you refuse to leave her alone. She must have one hell of a pussy because you keep going back."

In less than two seconds, I launched myself across the room and fisted his shirt in my hand. "Don't talk about her. Don't say her name. Don't even think her name." The minute I decided to go to war with Senator Deveron, I chose Hattie over everyone and everything, including my family, but I couldn't pretend I didn't feel divided by the whole thing. I had ripped my heart out of my chest and discarded the half belonging to my family. It sucked. "Do you understand?" I barked as I shoved him onto the sofa.

"You're making a mistake. A big fucking mistake."

My chest heaving, I glared at him as anger coursed through my nerve endings like a live wire.

"It's mine to make. I don't have to answer to you."

"You're right, you don't, but both of us know a woman like Hattie doesn't belong in our fucked up world. At least Anna knows what she's getting with me. She's a part of our world. Hattie doesn't have a clue. You'll break her."

I curled my hands into fists and stuffed them in my pockets so I didn't pummel him until he was bloody and bruised. He was right, and that thought made my hands tremble and my gut swirl with bile. Hattie had seen a glimpse of my world, but I'd sheltered her from darkest side of the Vargas Cartel while she was in Mexico. "I'm not part of your world."

He snorted as he shook his head. "You're lying to yourself if you believe you've washed your hands of the Vargas Cartel. It won't happen. Ignacio will find a way to reel you in, and once you're in, you're in for life. Trust me. I've experienced his twisted manipulations first hand. He'll fuck you five ways to Sunday without blinking an eye."

"He may screw up sometimes and be overbearing, but he loves you."

He raised his hands in the air. "If he loved me, he'd let me make my own decisions. Live my own life." He shook his head, his lips twisted into a distorted line. "Not even embezzling money or threatening to expose Ignacio's deals with corrupt politicians severed his hold on me. He's given you some breathing room, but it's all an illusion. He'll pull back the veil of compassion soon enough, and you'll end up just as bitter and fucked up as me."

I inhaled a deep breath, fighting back the

resentment hurling through my veins like acid at the thought of Ignacio sucking me into his world. "You don't know anything," I countered, even though I feared it might be the ugly truth. I fought fate for over a decade, and I had no intention of giving in any time soon.

"Fine, you keep living in your reality, and I'll live in mine. You might as well do it as long as you can." Rever turned up the volume on the television.

I stalked to the front door and snagged my personal phone off the entry table. "I'm going out. Clean up this shit and be in the guest room by the time I get back."

"Métetelo por el culo," Rever muttered under his breath, which roughly meant stick it up my ass.

I didn't respond. I didn't care. I didn't ask to be a participant in his life or his fucked up schemes. He asked me for a favor, not the other way around. *Entitled bastard.* I walked out the door without a second glance.

I hadn't changed my shirt or showered, which was my whole purpose in going home before I looked for Hattie. But right now, I couldn't stand another minute with Rever. He was right. We needed to make a plan to deal with Anna so he could get the fuck out of my place and move on with his life, preferably far away from me. Otherwise, we were going to kill each other.

Chapter Sixteen

Hattie

The Potomac River mirrored the color of the sky—dark stormy gray—just like my mood. It started sprinkling fifteen minutes ago, but I couldn't find the motivation to leave my park bench. Icy rain dribbled down my face and off my chin. My clothes were soaked, and shivers wracked my body, leaving me in a constant state of motion.

I'd roamed D.C. on foot for three hours after leaving Evan's place, and I still didn't understand. Nothing made sense. Not Evan. Not Ryker. Nothing. I felt like Dorothy in the Wizard of Oz when they pulled back the curtain and revealed a bunch of nonsense.

My phone rang in my purse nonstop for the last hour. Ryker was calling me. Vera never called. She texted. My mom and dad checked in with me once a week. If I didn't answer, they left a message.

At some point, I needed to answer his call, but I hadn't figured out what I wanted to say. I didn't own him. I couldn't ask him to change his life for me. Rationally, I should use his career to put a wedge between us, and walk away from him forever before everything exploded in my face.

I tried to unravel my feelings for Ryker.

Love.

Hate.

A perverse psychological attachment to my former captor.

Friendship.

Attraction.

A mixture of all of the above was probably the correct answer, but recognizing the complexity of my feelings didn't offer any enlightenment. Not really. Instead, the lead weight pressing against my chest felt heavier, suffocating me until I couldn't breathe. I'd done what thousands of women had done before. I fell for a man I believed would change and become somebody better for me. I pulled my legs to my chest and rested my head on my knees.

Gravel crunched behind me. The hair on the back of my neck stood on end. I didn't need to turn around to know Ryker was standing behind me. My body lit up like a stick of dynamite any time he came near me.

"Hattie?" he said in a hushed tone.

"I don't want to talk to you right now. Go away. I need to think," I mumbled without lifting my head. Just hearing the velvety rumble of his voice ignited a tug of war between hate and desire in my mind.

He dropped a black duffel bag on the end of a bench. "No," he answered without further explanation. He shook out a red and black plaid blanket and held it up in front of him like some sort of peace offering.

"I'm fine," I lied through chattering teeth.

"No, you're not. Your lips are blue, and your clothes are completely soaked."

I rolled my eyes. "Whatever." I snatched the blanket out of his hands and draped it over my shoulders.

He sat next to me and stretched out his long black-clad legs in front of him. His shirt highlighted the contours of his broad chest and narrow waist. His spicy sea-salt scent wafted into my lungs, and my heart skipped a beat or two.

He opened and closed his legs, pressing the length of his thigh into mine. Even that small, insignificant ghost of a touch made me want to forget everything Evan told me. I didn't trust myself to hold onto my anger long enough to confront him and hear his explanation.

Words spun wildly through my mind one after another, catching in my throat. I had so much to say and ask, but I didn't know where to start. I felt like I was crawling through a never-ending labyrinth, leading me to one dead end after another.

"How did you find me?"

He squeezed my arm. The subtle contact caused a fiery jolt of lust to rush through my arctic veins. "Process of elimination. You weren't at Vera's, the library, or my house. This park was the next stop on my list."

"Great. I'm predictable," I mumbled.

He smirked. "A little. I've noticed you like to

have a routine."

I nodded as I drew circles with the toe of my shoe in the mud.

"Where have you been all day?" he asked after an awkward pause. "You haven't answered my calls."

I stared forward, determined to ignore his piercing gaze. "What did you do today?" I snapped.

He slid his hand up and down my thigh. "I worked, but I already told you that this morning," he answered.

I glanced at him from the corner of my eye. "Worked? Does that mean you were busy making phone calls and raising funds for some illusive candidate?"

His hand paused mid-stroke. "No, but I think you already know that, or you wouldn't be asking me for details."

I turned my head to him and narrowed my eyes. "So you're not actually a campaign bundler."

"Sometimes, but I don't spend a lot of time doing it. I use the position to gather information about clients, people, and politicians. When I raise money for politicians, I discover a lot of information they'd prefer remained quiet."

I sucked in my lower lip. "So Evan wasn't lying. You are a political fixer."

He bent forward and rested his arms on his knees. "You saw Evan today?"

"Don't change the subject. Answer my question."

He rubbed his chin between his thumb and his index finger. "Yes. I'm a fixer of sorts. Not just for politicians though."

"Does that mean you get rid of dead bodies and beat people up?"

He flinched. "Not generally, but I'm not going to lie to you. My job isn't sunshine and roses."

My stomach rolled with acid. I closed my eyes, unable to look at him for another second. His strong fingers curled around my shoulders and he brushed his lips against mine, back and forth. Each touch sent equal frissons of lust and disgust zipping through my endorphin starved synapses.

"Look at me," he whispered, his warm minty breath wafted across my face.

"I can't." I shook my head and squeezed my eyes tighter. I couldn't look at his face. I was afraid I'd see a depraved monster instead of the man I craved more than my next breath. *What did it say about me if I was falling in love with a terrible person?*

He kissed one eyelid and then the other. Fire and passion sparked inside my heart. I tried to stifle the hitch in my breath, but it sounded like a moan.

"You can't what?" he asked.

"I don't know if I want to be with you. You're no better than Evan and his dad. No, you're worse. You're the hired muscle beating the weak and vulnerable into submission for a bunch of shady assholes."

Ryker chuckled, and my eyes popped open. "Trust me, Hattie. Nobody I deal with is weak or vulnerable. Far from it. More like corrupted and greedy, sometimes worse. Much worse."

I frowned. "And that makes everything okay in your mind."

He lips curled into a half smile. "It makes my job palatable."

My eyes trailed down his body and back up again. I studied him, scrutinizing every twitch in his jaw, move of his mouth, and the tilt of his chin. I counted the number of times he blinked. I evaluated the size of his pupils and the contours of his forearms. For some unfathomable reason, I believed I'd find the answers to all my questions hidden somewhere in the depths of his face. I found nothing. A vacant mask. An empty wall. How could he conceal his emotions so easily? Mine bled out of my pores, announcing everything as effectively as broadcasting them through a bullhorn.

"What's that?" I pointed to rust-colored flecks on his shirt resembling bloodstains.

He glanced at his shirt and dropped his hands from my shoulders. "A hard day at work."

Disgusted with him and myself, I ripped the blanket off my shoulders and tossed it at his face. My frustration wasn't limited to his career choice. He had kept me in the dark, hiding the rest of his life from me, lying until he thought he could trust me with the truth, or maybe he hoped he'd never have to tell me. Instead, Evan told me, which doubled the betrayal.

"I'm going home. I'll call you tomorrow." I stood and broke into a jog, knowing I wouldn't be able to maintain my composure for much longer. He lunged for me, but I evaded him with a last minute sidestep.

In all honesty, I didn't know where I planned to go, much less sleep at night. I didn't want to see

Vera yet. I hadn't determined the extent of her role in Evan's scheming. The email didn't confirm or deny her complicity. Instead, it made me second-guess everything. Until I had more information, I wouldn't step foot in her apartment again, which meant I had to check into a hotel because my parents' house wasn't an option. Dealing with my mom right now would send me into a tailspin. One needling comment and I'd explode.

I darted through the trees, and away from the man who turned me inside out with nothing more than a smile or a fleeting glance. Water seeped through the holes of my laser-cut leather ballet flats. Mud splashed my pants. I nearly slipped on the wet grass more than once, but I kept putting one foot in front of the other, determined to put as much time and space between Ryker and me as possible. If I concentrated hard enough, I could pretend the last three months hadn't happened.

That he wasn't following me.

That he'd let me go.

That everything would right itself, and I'd be happy again.

"Hattie," Ryker said, enveloping my hips with his large hands and yanking my back against his chest. The warmth of his body penetrated my soaked shirt. The steady beat of his heart drummed against my spine. My eyelids slid closed in dismay. His warm breath tickled my ear, and my entire body stiffened, every bitterly cold muscle in my body coiling tighter and tighter. The chaotic buzzing in my head got louder and louder as my jumbled desires swirled relentlessly through my mind.

"Let me go." Tears bled from the corners of my eyes, and sadness rippled in tiny waves through my soul. "Please, just let me go. I'm not playing this game with you today. Okay?" I pleaded weakly, my voice wavering.

He tightened his grip on my hips, and electric sparks shot through his fingertips, igniting my barely suppressed yearning for him. "No, you're upset, you're soaking wet, and it's dark. I'm not letting you wander the city right now, regardless of whether you think I'm playing games with you."

I cradled my head in my hands as a veil of lust whirled around us. I mentally sliced it into a million jagged pieces, desperately searching for any remnants of my common sense. How could I feel so close to him yet so far from him all at once? How could I want him but hate him?

"I had a bad day. I don't want to fight with you today. I need some space to get my thoughts together. I'm not running away."

"Listen," he whispered as he tangled his fingers in my hair, brushing it away from my face. "I'm not a hit man, and I generally don't go around beating up people. What happened today was unusual. For the most part, I analyze the numbers, secure waivers from legislation, make ominous phone calls, raise the money, covertly manage or redirect the media, and facilitate the consummation or destruction of deals."

"Is everything you do legal?"

"I won't lie, some of it steps over the line, but as of today it's all in the past. I don't want to do it anymore. I haven't in a long time. I don't need the money, and I don't want the headache anymore. It's over, okay?"

I dropped my hands, and they swayed like tumbleweed against my legs. "You don't have to quit for me. We're just…" My voice trailed off, and I shrugged. I didn't know how to define our relationship. We were so many things—all of them contradictory, like a string of double negatives. In the end, they canceled each other out, but instead of equaling a positive, we were left with a void. "We're nothing," I mumbled, and my lungs contracted in my chest, my entire being objecting to my declaration. I was screwed up, and I didn't know if I'd ever be normal again.

"We're a lot of things, but nothing isn't one of them." His low, velvety voice caressed me like an embrace. Shivers danced down my spine, begging me to turn around and kiss him. Devour him. Take what he offered while I still had the chance.

I groaned, curling my hands into fists and leaning into him. My body was at war, craving him and hating him. "It should be the only thing," I countered.

Sensing my capitulation, he twirled me around and trailed kisses along my neck. "Nothing has changed since last night. Don't run away now." He tilted my head up, searching my face for something. Forgiveness? "Tell me I didn't ruin this, ruin us," he whispered next to my ear, his voice raw and needy.

I cursed my body as I slanted into him and angled my head to the side, inviting his touch. "Everything has changed."

"How?"

"I went to see Evan today."

Twin lines marred the skin between his eyebrows and lines bracketed his mouth. His gray eyes glowed like moonstones. "I warned you to stay away from him and Senator Deveron. Nothing good will come out of confronting them. We need a plan."

A strangled sob tumbled from my lips. "I had to talk to him. I had to know."

His fingertips dug into my arms. "You had to know what?"

"Why he did it. If I ever meant anything to him. If our relationship had been a game from the very beginning."

He sighed as he shook his head. "And what did you find out?"

I swallowed and fixed my gaze on the tree behind him. "He has a private investigator following me."

He brushed his fingers along my jaw line and then along my cheek, sweeping away my tears.

"I know," he admitted.

I frowned. "How did you know?"

"He hired them before you went to Mexico. I didn't know for sure, but I assumed he still had someone following you, especially after you ended the engagement."

"Vera helped him too." I bit the corner of my lower lip. "Well, I'm not sure exactly what she did. Do you know anything about that?"

"No." He shook his head. "If she helped him, neither he nor Senator Deveron mentioned anything to me. She might have helped in a non-material way, but I don't think she knows anything. I doubt they'd confide in her. It'd be too risky."

Relief surged through my veins. "I guess you're right, but it's hard to believe in anyone now."

"You can believe in me," he rasped, resting his forehead against mine.

I wiped my nose with the back of my hand as uneven sobs fled the safety of my mouth. "Can I? Because I'm not sure I should trust anyone."

His eyes locked on mine, brown colliding with gray, and all the emotions I'd been sidestepping for the past twenty minutes sizzled shamelessly. Invisible silken webs coiled around us, shackling us together in a cloud of lust. My nipples hardened. Sweltering desire pumped through my blood, thawing my frozen limbs. No amount of mental imagery could walk me back from the abyss.

Cold hands framed my face. "You can, but I realize I have to earn your trust. Just give me enough time to do it." He ghosted a soft kiss across my lips, and his eyes crinkled at the corners. "I have never wanted a woman as much as I want you. I know I should do the right thing and walk away and let you live your life far away from me, but when it comes to you, I never do the right thing. I need every part of you, and someday you'll give it to me. Freely and without reservations. Until then, I'll take what you're willing to give."

"Okay," I whispered, leaning into him, capitalizing on the safety of his embrace.

His familiar scent of spice and sea-salt bewitched me. I wanted to be closer to him. Feel him. Touch him. Taste him. I wanted to have a reason to live and love instead of feeling numb, betrayed, and bitter. I yanked his shirt from his waistband and slipped my fingers beneath his shirt. The pads of my icy fingers traced the rope-like muscles lining his spine. Up and down. Down and up.

Ryker sucked in a breath, and his fingers trailed from my neck to my shoulders, and then down my arms. My heart tattooed the inside of my chest. His eyes held me hostage. I couldn't look away. Out of everything that had happened over the past three months, Ryker was the one reason I'd do it all again without a second thought.

The pain.

The confusion.

The betrayals.

The anger.

Finding him, loving him was worth it. In that instant, I discarded my thoughts of leaving him. I abandoned every notion of turning my back on us. Of all the twisted emotions I felt for Ryker, my love for him screamed the loudest. Fought the hardest.

Without saying a word, he scooped me up in one smooth motion and half ran, half walked, stopping only to grab his bag and blanket from the park bench.

"Where are we going?" I asked as I dotted his neck with open-mouthed kisses.

"To my car."

I laughed. "Thank God. I'm freezing my ass off."

"You're the one who refused my blanket," he said as he wrenched his car door open and laid me down in the backseat.

"I was upset," I said with a smirk.

He shook his head as he climbed into the backseat with me.

He started unbuttoning my shirt.

"What are you doing?" I asked, my eyes locked on his skillful fingers as he opened my shirt button by button and peeled it off my body. He traced the scalloped edge of my bra, painting invisible lines all over my skin. My muscles jumped under his fingertips. He was the pied piper, and I couldn't stop my body from marching to his tune.

"Getting you out of these clothes," he answered. His lips curled into a lopsided grin, and my heart screeched to a halt. His hands moved to my jeans, and in less than thirty seconds, I was stretched out on the smooth leather in nothing but my panties and bra.

"You know what?" I asked with my eyebrows raised.

"What?" he said absently as his eyes roamed over my body, drinking me in like a man who had finished a trek through the Sahara.

My hands moved to the collar of his shirt. I flicked one button open, then two and three. My hands kept moving until I parted his shirt, exposing his golden skin and his beautifully defined chest and stomach. "I think your clothes are a little wet too."

He bent forward as I pushed his shirt from his shoulder. "You're right. I think we both would benefit from sharing body heat," he murmured right before his warm lips crushed against mine.

Our tongues tangled. Our mouths fused together. Our hands clawed at anything in our way.

Tasting.

Savoring.

Devouring.

Exploring.

Each additional piece of clothing we removed was like tinder feeding the bonfire of lust raging between us. Moans and whimpers harmonized with the pinging sound of the rain as it splattered against the car. Our skin stuck together from a combination of water and sweat as our bodies slid against each other.

I didn't care that we were cramped together in the backseat of his car in a parking lot of a public park. I didn't care that my life was spinning out of control at an alarming velocity. My need for control vanished whenever he was near me. Good or bad—I didn't know, but it was the unvarnished truth, and I loved and hated it.

With fumbling hands, I shoved his pants down his legs, exposing the sharp angle of muscles adjacent to his hipbone. I traced the sculpted line to his erection.

"You make me crazy," he whispered as his lips nipped, sucked, and kissed their way to my breasts. He sucked a hardened nipple into his mouth, and a burst of pleasure shot through my body.

I moaned, arching into him as I slid my hand along his length. Up and down, I caressed him as I alternated between watching his face and the glide of my hand. "I do?" My voiced sounded throaty and totally unlike me, which was fitting because I didn't feel like myself around him. Instead of a controlled, principled person, I morphed into an adrenaline junkie ruled by impulses, emotions, and lust.

He rested his forehead against mine, his chest heaving. He stared at me as if he had summoned me by wishing on a shooting star. "You know you do. From the minute I saw you in that bar, I knew I had a problem. Maybe before then."

I chuckled. "Good, because I suspected you were trouble."

I pushed his chest. "Sit up," I demanded.

"Not yet." He smirked as his fingers traced the opening of my sex.

"Oh God," I murmured. Each teasing motion of his finger intensified the needy ache in my core. Lifting my hips, I rocked against his hand wanting more, each languid circle of his finger more intense than the previous one.

Flushed and shaking, I mumbled hundreds of incoherent thoughts about needing him, wanting him, craving him, and not being able to live without him. Just as flames started rolling through me, he jerked his hand away from where I needed him. My eyes popped open.

"What the—"

His damp fingers rested against my lips, slowly moving back and forth. "Shh, I'll take care of you." He lifted me up, so I straddled his waist. "Do you want to do this here?"

At a loss for words, I nodded urgently, up and down like a bobble head doll. I would've laughed at myself if I wasn't so focused on feeling him inside of me. In seconds, he grabbed my hips, rotating them back and forth over the tip of his erection.

"Please," I whimpered.

"Guide me inside of you," he responded, his

voice gruff and uncontrolled. I liked him that way.

I angled my body, and he sunk deep inside of me. I groaned as I grinded against him. He curled his fingers around my hips as his mouth collided with mine—a messy, wet combination of teeth, tongue, and lips.

"Fuck," he muttered, slanting his head, breaking our kiss, and burying his head next to my neck. "This isn't going to last." He trailed open-mouthed kisses up and down my neck and behind my ear, sending tremors down my spine. Our bodies glistened with sweat and rain. Our exhalations fogged the windows as we rocked against each other, his hips colliding with mine.

He pushed me back against the seat, tilted my hips up, and slammed back inside of me. A jagged groan exploded from my mouth. "Oh God, right there."

He gripped my hips, using them as leverage as he pounded inside of me. My head tapped against the door with every thrust. Delicious embers of pleasure spiraled through my body. I dug my fingers into his hips, forcing him to move faster, harder, and burying himself deeper until I felt boneless and complete.

I sunk my hands into his hair, pulling him closer. His lips crashed against mine, our moans and gasps tangled and danced until they became one stream ping-ponging back and forth between our mouths. Each flex and rotation of his hips lured me closer and closer to the finish line. Then, a bright light flashed behind my eyelids, and a cyclone of bliss whirled through me as all my nerve endings fired in a chorus of Hallelujahs.

After one final thrust, he tensed and then collapsed on top of me, his chest heaving and my legs still twisted around his waist. Our hearts thumped against each other as I smoothed my fingers through his damp hair.

"Maybe we should have waited," he whispered next to my ear.

"No. That was…perfect."

A strangled chuckle escaped his lips, tickling the side of my neck. "Perfect, huh?" He braced his body on his elbows, his eyes searching mine with a faint smile on his too sexy lips. "I don't think anyone has ever called car sex perfect."

I laughed. "Maybe you're right."

He swept my hair from my face. "No more secrets. No more lies. No more running."

I nodded as hope bloomed in my heart. Maybe we could do this. Really do this. Together. With nothing between us.

"We should go before…" His voice trailed off and he shrugged.

I sat up and gathered my wet clothes. "No, you're right."

He unzipped his black duffel and handed me a t-shirt and gym shorts. "Here, put these on."

I eyed them suspiciously.

"They're clean," he said, pulling on his pants and fastening them.

I shrugged and then put them on before I climbed into the front seat. A few seconds later, he joined me. He didn't start the car right away. Instead, he stared out the front windshield as he drummed his fingers on the steering wheel, darkness bathing the interior of the car.

"We didn't use a condom again," he finally said, not looking at me.

I swallowed hard. "I know." It didn't cross my mind until he said it, but I never thought clearly around him. "I still haven't had my period."

"I think you should go to the doctor."

Alarm constricted my chest. He was right. I'd been thinking the same thing, but I spent the last few weeks concentrating on everything and anything but the giant elephant in the room. "Maybe."

He squeezed my leg, attempting to reassure me. "Hey."

I turned to face him. "Yeah?"

He turned on the ignition. "Either way it will be okay. Trust me, we'll figure it out."

I blew out a breath and nodded my head. "You're right. It's not the end of the world."

He turned on the car and pulled out of the parking lot. "Not even close," he said so softly I almost missed it.

Chapter Seventeen

Ryker

After Hattie had fallen asleep, I snuck into the guest room to talk to Rever. I wanted to move forward with Hattie, but in order to make it happen, I needed to get Rever out of my apartment and my life. I couldn't procrastinate any longer. As much as I'd like to ignore it, we had to address the Anna situation.

Rever wasn't asleep. He was leaning against the headboard with his iPad in his lap.

"Are you busy?" I asked, closing the door softly behind me.

"Does it look like it?" he snapped without meeting my eyes.

Ignoring his comment, I settled into the chair in the corner of the room. The tension had grown steadily between us with every passing day. "What do you want to do about Anna?"

He tossed his iPad on the top of the bed. "Does this mean you're finally ready to help?"

I tapped my fingers on the arm of the chair,

trying to control my temper. Rever acted like a petulant child when he didn't get his way. "It depends on the circumstances. I'm not going on a suicide mission, but if there's a logical way to get her, then I'll help you. I won't do it alone though."

Rever sat up and dangled his legs over the side of the bed. "She goes to church every Sunday. *El Sagrado Corazón de Jesús*. That's the only time she's allowed to leave their home."

"Are you suggesting we abduct her from the church? Should we storm the church with our guns and drag her out of there?" I mocked.

"No. She could pretend she didn't feel well and walk outside during mass. We'd be waiting by the curb."

"And then where do we go?"

"We should leave by helicopter, not a boat. A boat would take too long."

I nodded absently. "Whose helicopter? We can't ask anyone associated with Ignacio or the Vargas Cartel."

Rever shrugged. "I have a friend who runs a helicopter tour service out of Cancun. I think he'd help us."

I scrubbed my hands over my face. "Is he trustworthy?"

"I trust him. He's a good guy. We've been friends for over ten years."

I raised my eyebrows in disbelief. Being friends with Rever for over a decade wasn't exactly a ringing endorsement of trustworthiness. From what Ignacio told me, Rever spent the last ten years drinking, taking drugs, and fucking.

Rever stood up and shook his head. "I know what you're thinking, but Emilio is a good guy. He's not like me. He has a wife and a couple of kids. He's spent the last five years building his business. He's bailed me out of more than one bad situation over the years."

"I don't know, Rever. Have you thought this through?" I pinched the bridge of my nose. "Think about what you're saying. Do you really think it's a good idea to involve someone with a wife and kids?"

His brows snapped together, and he frowned. "What do you mean?"

"If we're successful and Juan Alvarez finds out about his involvement, we're basically painting a giant crosshair on Emilio's forehead. They'd slaughter him along with every member of his family." I raised my eyebrows. "Are you okay with that?"

Rever paced the length of the room and back again. "I realize that, but I'll pay him enough to make it worth the risk. He can take his family and move across the country and start a whole new life. Change his name. Start a new business. Any business he wanted."

My eyes narrowed, and I rubbed my temples. Ten minutes of talking to Rever and my head already felt like exploding. His idea was crazy. Rever would need to pay him a shit ton of money to risk crossing the Alvarez Cartel. "Ignacio cut off your access to funds. Where are you going to get that kind of money, because I'm sure as hell not going to loan it to you?"

"I've put some things into motion, and if all goes well, I should have plenty of money within the next day or two." He lifted one shoulder. "I'll be set for a couple of years even after I pay Emilio."

I groaned and dropped my head into my hands. My headache just magnified tenfold. "Fuck, Rever. What did you do?"

He folded his arms across his chest, drumming his fingers on his biceps. "Don't worry about it. The less you know, the better. Let me take care of the money, and you can plan the operation. I'll give you Emilio's number. He's waiting for your call."

Tugging at the roots of my hair, I pushed out of my chair. "No. Tell me everything or I'm not helping you."

Anything involving that kind of money was illegal as fuck. Rever didn't have a track record of success when it came to making plans. His money-laundering scheme in Las Vegas landed his ass in jail, and that wasn't the first mess Ignacio and I had to clean up.

"No. I can't. I don't want to involve you in the details. If I go down, I don't want to drag you with me."

I chuckled, but it lacked mirth. There were a number of reasons why he wouldn't want me to be implicated, but none of them involved concern for my welfare. More likely, he wanted someone on the outside to get him out if he was arrested again, or he thought I'd stop his harebrained idea in its tracks. Rever never cared about anyone except himself. He believed the world revolved around him, which made me question why he gave a shit about Anna and his unborn child. It certainly didn't make sense.

"I became involved the minute you showed up at my apartment. In case you've forgotten already, you agreed to leave the U.S. and never come back as a condition of your release a month ago."

"It's better this way."

"Then, you need to leave. I'm done helping you." I crossed the room and opened the door.

"Where I am supposed to go?"

Weariness settled into my bones, and I didn't bother turning around. The day when I no longer had to deal with the Vargas Cartel or Rever couldn't come fast enough. "I don't care, just be gone by tomorrow morning."

"Wait." He grabbed my shoulder.

"What?"

"Fine. I'll tell you everything, but it's already in motion so I can't stop it now."

I closed the door softly and turned to face him, folding my arms across my chest. "Go ahead, and don't leave out a single detail. I don't want to be ambushed later. If you lie, I'll take you down myself."

Rever dragged his hand through his hair. "I arranged a shipment of ten pounds of crystal meth and five kilos of heroin to be transported to the D.C. area."

"How did you pay for it?"

"I paid for it before I came to the U.S." Rever sucked in a deep breath. "I suspected Ignacio would shut down my accounts the minute he realized I left Mexico."

"So you had this planned from the very

beginning and you never intended to tell me about it."

He ran a hand over his mouth as he shifted his weight from one foot to the other. "I did, but with good reason."

"Dammit, Rever," I spat, anger coursing like poison through my veins. I wanted to rip him apart piece by piece. He was reckless, even more so than I remembered. He may have stopped using drugs, but his judgment hadn't improved. "I wouldn't have let you stay here if I'd known you were involved in a freelance trafficking scheme."

"I know, but you were my only option."

"Did you use Ignacio's people to supply you the drugs?"

He cringed. "Yes."

"Ignacio will find out."

"I know he will, but the deal will be done by then, and there won't be anything he can do about it."

I balled my hands into fists. "Except take revenge."

Rever shrugged. "They knew the risks."

I shook my head. "How are you moving the drugs across the border?"

"One of Ignacio's tunnels."

My eyebrows jumped up my forehead. "Seriously?"

"Did you expect me to make a deal with a rival cartel?" he snapped. "I didn't have much time. I used the resources and contacts at my disposal."

This plan had disaster written all over it. Rever had to trust a shitload of people not to double-cross or blackmail him in order for this plan to succeed. "How are you distributing it?"

"The Mexican Mafia."

"Wow," I said as I cocked my head to the side. "This is a bad fucking idea. The Mexican Mafia is unpredictable."

Rever rolled his eyes, trying to brush off my criticism, but I could see his anger. His shoulders tensed, and his jaw muscles twitched. "They won't cross me. I've done this a few times before, and they know what happens if they snitch or fail to pay."

I snorted. "So this is a consistent side job for you?"

"Look." He raised his hands in front of his chest. "I've done it two or three times in the past. It gave me an income independent from Ignacio and the Vargas Cartel."

"That's what jobs are for."

"Don't lecture me. You're basically a political hit man."

I slapped my open hand on top of the dresser. "I don't kill people."

"I don't believe you, and you know what? I don't give a shit how you earn your money, but don't judge me. If you'd grown up under Ignacio's thumb, you wouldn't have a third of the freedoms you had growing up or even now. He'd be riding your ass every day about every small detail like he still does with me."

I gritted my teeth. I didn't want to have this conversation with Rever. He blamed Ignacio for every perceived slight. He needed to start taking responsibility for his actions instead of using the victim card at every opportunity.

"When are you supposed to get the money?" I asked, purposely changing the subject.

"The drugs have already been delivered to the Mexican Mafia, and they're supposed to pay me tomorrow or the next day. Then, I'm done. I should net over a million and half dollars."

"How are you getting the money?"

"They're wiring some of the money to various accounts I've set up around the world. Panama. Andorra. Cayman Islands. Just to name a few. Then, I have a contact who will exchange the rest of the money for gold and diamonds. I'll trade the gold and diamonds for cash in Panama and buy a house for Anna and me."

I nodded absently. He described the two most common techniques for laundering money. "Are you meeting with the Mexican Mafia again?"

Rever yanked on the collar of his t-shirt. "No. We're done. All the arrangements have been made."

I blew out a breath and took a couple of steps to the door. "It's almost morning. I'm going back to bed."

He cleared his throat. "You're still going to help me, right?"

"I can't talk about this anymore. I need to cool off first and wrap my head around everything you told me. Go to bed, and we'll talk in the morning." I cracked open the door.

"Am I allowed out of my room?"

I glanced over my shoulder with narrowed eyes. "What's that supposed to mean?"

"Princess Hattie is sleeping over tonight, right?"

"What are you getting at?"

"You don't want us to meet."

I leaned my shoulder into the doorjamb. "You're right, but it's unavoidable. She's going to be staying here for a while. Just leave her alone, and you can stay here."

"*Qué chingados?*" he growled, his nostrils flaring. "You can't trust her with all the shit going down right now. You hardly know her." He shook his head. "It's crazy. She could turn on you in a second and sing like a canary to every government agency under the sun."

I spun around. My hands clenched, I prowled forward until I stood inches from his face. I shoved my palm against his chest, and he stumbled backward, bumping into the edge of the mattress. I wanted to hit him, but I smothered the urge. Giving Rever a black eye or a bloody nose wouldn't solve anything. Besides, he'd fight back, and I didn't want to wake Hattie up because I couldn't keep my fists to myself.

"*¡Cállate!*" I yelled, switching to Spanish.

"*Bastardo,*" he hissed as he grabbed my wrist and pushed my hand away from him. "*No me toques.*"

"I don't care what you want or don't want. Don't talk about Hattie. Don't talk to Hattie. You got that? You don't know anything about her. Don't pretend otherwise."

He breathed hard through his nose, and his chest heaved with barely concealed rage. "She'll complicate everything. You know it, and I know it."

"Yeah, well, so did your dumbass relationship with Anna. If you'd stayed away from her and kept your dick in your pants, we wouldn't be in this mess."

I walked out of the room without waiting for his answer. He'd never admit any wrongdoing, and he'd never apologize unless I held a gun to his head.

Chapter Eighteen

Hattie

I woke to the sound of hushed voices outside of Ryker's bedroom. I couldn't make out any of the words, which meant he didn't want me to overhear the conversation. Resting on my elbows, I stared at the ceiling and the walls, absorbing the minimal details of his bedroom. Similar to the rest of his apartment, it didn't have any personal effects.

No pictures.

No artwork.

No books or scattered papers.

Just the bare necessities.

Would Ryker always be a mystery? Occasionally, I glimpsed pieces of him beneath his mask, but as quickly as those moments materialized, they disappeared. Just as I thought I'd gained ground, something happened to make me realize I didn't know much of anything. I shook my head to dispel my morose thoughts. Things were getting better.

When the voices faded, I jumped out of bed and

snagged one of his dress shirts from the hanger in his closet. I buttoned it enough to cover me, and combed my fingers through my tangled hair. I hadn't been back to the apartment I shared with Vera for two days, and I didn't have anything to wear except for the few things I snagged from Evan's place.

My phone vibrated on the nightstand. I picked it up and read the message.

Vera: Where are you? You haven't been home in two nights. Your mom and dad are blowing up my phone and threatening to come over.

I rolled my eyes. My mom must have received news of my fight with Evan. She probably wanted to have a family meeting to discuss my obligations as a member of the Covington family. Fuck her.

Me: I'm fine. I'll be back later today.

Vera responded immediately.

Vera: Okay. Can you call your mom? I'd prefer to stay out of her line of fire. She's on the warpath. What the hell did you do?

I groaned. A couple of months ago, I would've shared all the sordid details of my relationship with Ryker, but now I didn't know if I could trust her. In a matter of months, I went from having a best friend, a serious boyfriend, and an organized, predictable life to total chaos. Even crazier, I wouldn't change anything. I was hopelessly drawn to Ryker, inextricably caught in his web for better or for worse. My soul had chosen him. I didn't have a choice.

Me: Who knows? I'll call her. Don't answer her calls. You don't need to deal with her.

I sat crossed-legged in the middle of Ryker's bed as I scrolled through my missed calls. Five from my mom last night and one from my dad an hour ago. If I could find any way to avoid calling her, I would.

I slammed my finger on her contact. Unfortunately for me, she answered after the first ring.

"Hattie, where the hell are you?"

"I'm getting ready to go on a run. What do you want?" I responded after a lengthy pause. It was a lie, but the truth wasn't necessary.

I heard her heels, clicking on the tile floor. I guess she needed some privacy to say what she wanted.

"Can you meet me for coffee around the corner from my house in the next twenty minutes?" Her voice was hushed.

I lifted my chin and closed my eyes briefly. "I don't know. I just woke up."

"Thirty minutes, then? Is that long enough? This is really important. We need to talk."

I grabbed my purse off the dresser and pulled some clothes from my purse. I cringed. They were damp and hopelessly wrinkled. "Fine. I'll do my best."

When I walked out of Ryker's bedroom, his apartment was empty. I spotted a note on the kitchen counter.

Hattie,

I'll be back by noon. Breakfast is in the refrigerator. Call me if you leave.

Ryker

I picked up the pen sitting next to the note and then set it back down. I'd planned to beat him back here anyway. I didn't need to leave a note.

***

Forty minutes later, I walked into the coffee shop. The rich smell of coffee flooded my nose. My mom sat in the back corner with huge sunglasses covering her eyes and her hair styled into an elegant twist. Unlike me, her light gray suit was pressed.

"Hi, mom," I said as I pressed a kiss to her plastic cheek.

Her eyes swept down my body. "You look…tired."

I shrugged as I slipped into the chair across from her. "It's been a rough couple of days."

She gestured to her cup of tea. She didn't drink coffee. She drank herbal tea, preferably organic and single-estate. "Do you want something to drink?"

"Maybe later."

She removed her sunglasses and placed them on the table. "Did you get everything settled with your professors?"

I leaned back in my chair. "Yes, but I'm pretty sure I told you that last week."

She glanced at the exit. "You're probably right." She tapped her sunglasses against the table. "How do you like living with Vera?"

"It's okay."

She nodded, her teeth nearly splintering under the weight of her counterfeit smile. "That's nice." She twirled her mug on the table, then she lifted it to her lips. "You know, you can move home. We'd be happy to have you. You can even take the apartment over the garage, so you have some personal space."

I folded my arms across my chest. "Mom, what do you want? What's really going on?"

She exhaled shakily and set her mug on the table again. "Evan called your dad last night."

I raised one eyebrow. "Oh, really?"

"He's worried about you," she whispered as she slanted her body against the table.

I snorted. "I don't give a shit about Evan. In fact, I'd appreciate it if you'd stop talking to him."

Her light pink lipstick disappeared as she pressed her lips into an unyielding line. "I can't do that. The Deverons are family friends. Very close family friends. We have a special relationship," she hissed. "Just because you and Evan pressed the pause button on your engagement doesn't mean I'm going to kick him or his family out of our life on a whim. That would be awkward when you get back together."

I rolled my eyes. She was so predictable. "I

didn't press the pause button. I ended the engagement." I unfolded my arms and gripped the edge of the table. "It's over. Stop pretending otherwise. I hate him. I hate that I wasted so many years with him. I hate that I accepted his engagement in a moment of weakness. I don't want anything to do with him."

"You don't mean that. You're overly emotional. You're still recovering from the…" Unwilling to complete the sentence, she waved her hand in front of me.

"Abduction. Is that the word you're looking for?"

She nodded. "Yes, and that's why I wanted to talk to you. We're going on a family retreat with the Deverons next weekend."

"You and dad?"

"All of us."

"No way. I'm not going," I snapped.

"Yes, you will." Her lips pursed in disapproval. "It's been arranged. It'd look bad if you didn't come."

"I don't care how it looks. They fucked up my entire life. They arranged my abduction. Does that change your mind? Or are you too worried about screwing up your social calendar to care what they did to me?" The minute the words exited my mouth, I wanted to shove them back. I'd never been good at confronting my mom. As a child, I had rebelled in subtle ways, plotting my time until I could escape from her sphere of influence. She wasn't used to open rebellion.

Her mouth dropped open. "What are you talking

about? That doesn't make sense."

I squeezed my hands into fists. "Forget about it. Forget I said anything. I'm fine. Everything's fine. I've never been better." I picked up my purse from the chair next to me and slammed it on the table. "Are we done here?"

"Oh my God, Evan was right. He was telling the truth." She covered her mouth, and her eyes flared with panic.

My heart galloped, and my shoulder muscles contracted into tight balls. "What did he say?"

"He said he thought you were suffering from…" Her voice faded away, and the silence stretched like hours instead of a few meager seconds. Then, she cleared her throat. "Traumatic bonding."

My stomach contorted into a hundred tiny acid-filled knots. "Traumatic bonding?" I repeated.

"You know…Stockholm syndrome. When a victim becomes attached to her captor. He said you've been defending and rationalizing the actions of your captors."

I glared at her, resentment whipping through my veins. She actually believed his lies. "Evan doesn't know anything. He's a liar. Why would you believe him? Why would you take his side?"

With her eyes narrowed in thought, she studied me like she didn't recognize the person in front of her. "I'm on your side. I'm always on your side. That's why I'm here. I want to make sure you're happy and healthy."

"You want me to be happy?" She nodded, and I shifted in my seat. "Great, then stop pushing me to reconcile with Evan. He's not who you think he is.

His dad isn't either."

"Evan said you're blaming him for what happened."

"If the shoe fits," I spat.

"He thinks you're still communicating with someone in the Vargas Cartel and that person is influencing your actions."

I scrubbed my hands over my face. So this was his plan. Evan thought he could make my family believe I had lost my mind. "Mom, do me a favor. When you want to know the truth, call me." I snatched my purse from the table. "Until then, we're done talking."

She grabbed my wrist. "Are you coming next weekend? I think it'd be nice for us to spend time together."

"No, but you can give Evan and his dad a message from me."

Her brows furrowed. "What's that?"

"Tell them they won't get away with what they did to me, and I have every intention of exposing Senator Deveron."

She shook her head back and forth. "That sounds crazy, Hattie. Is that some kind of threat?"

"It's not a threat." I ripped my wrist away from her. "It's a promise. If you pulled your head out of Senator Deveron's ass for a few seconds and opened your eyes, you'd realize you need to be far, far away from him. It's only a matter of time before his corruption is exposed."

My whole life, I had waited with baited breath for my mom to believe in me and support me 100 percent, but I was starting to realize it'd never happen. She second-guessed every decision I made. She treated me like a naughty toddler instead of an adult with dreams and goals. Her inability to let go of my relationship with Evan had gone on long enough. If she wanted me in her life, she had to choose my dreams over hers.

"Don't go. Let's talk about this. You can't make those kinds of accusations and run away. Maybe you should come over tonight and talk to your dad about some of your concerns."

"Let me know when you're ready to listen to the truth, and if dad wants to call me, he has my number. Goodbye, mother."

Chapter Nineteen

Hattie

At exactly 11:45 a.m., I tried to turn the door handle to Ryker's apartment. I didn't have a key, so I'd left it unlocked. If he found out he wouldn't be happy, but he lived in a secured building, and I hadn't been gone long.

The handle didn't move. *Shit.* Ryker beat me home. I slipped my phone from my purse, checking for any missed voicemails or texts. None. He hadn't attempted to contact me.

I balled my hand into a fist and tapped on the heavy, dark wood door, lightly at first and then harder when no one answered. The thud echoed down the long hallway.

Just when I had decided to give up and call Ryker, the door opened.

"Who are you? Where's Ryker?" I glanced over his shoulder, but I didn't see Ryker.

"You weren't supposed to leave without calling Ryker," the man said, a faint accent flavoring his words.

"How do you know that?"

He tilted his head to the side and smirked. "I read the note."

"Great, and who are you?" I asked, repeating my question. His dark eyes and his angular nose looked familiar, but I hadn't met him before.

"Ryker's brother." His dark hooded eyes swept down my body. "And you're Hattie Covington."

The minute he revealed his connection to Ryker, I couldn't deny the family resemblance between Ignacio and Rever, and to a lesser extent, Ryker. His face was fuller than Ignacio's, and he wasn't as tall as Ryker, but they all shared the same nose and eye shape. I backpedaled a few steps. "I didn't realize you were still living here."

He turned away, leaving the door open for me. "Ryker doesn't let me come out to play when you're around. He likes to keep me locked away in the guest bedroom."

"Why's that?" I asked, closing the door behind me.

He plopped down onto the sofa, stretching his legs out on the coffee table. "Who knows? Maybe he doesn't want to upset your delicate sensibilities. Maybe he thinks you'll like me better."

I rolled my eyes. "I don't think he has to worry about that." I walked into the kitchen and pulled a bottle of water out of the refrigerator.

He scoffed in disbelief, but otherwise ignored the comment. "By the way, he should be back any minute. He decided to cut his day short when he found out you left without calling him."

I bristled as I leaned against the wall and took a

sip of water. "How does he know I left?"

Rever snickered. "I called him."

My brows snapped together. "Why would you do that?"

"For some dumb reason he thinks he can trust you. I wanted him to know he can't."

I squeezed my bottle of water, forcing myself to stay calm and unaffected by his words. "You don't know me."

He scowled. "I don't know you, but I know all about you. You're just another entitled bitch who thinks everything revolves around you, but you don't know shit about living in the real world. The minute things get complicated, you're going to run to your daddy and confess everything, and in the process you will ruin my brother's life."

I folded my arms across my chest and raised one eyebrow. "And he can trust you? The man who stole from his family. The man who planned to sell out his dad in exchange for prosecutorial immunity. The man who abandoned his pregnant girlfriend in Mexico because he didn't want to deal with his dad. I think not."

Rever jumped up, his hands curled into balls. "Shut the fuck up. None of this is your business."

"It became my business the minute your actions fucked up my life. You're a selfish prick who doesn't care about anyone."

A vein pulsed in the side of his neck. "You don't know anything about me."

"Oh really," I said. "Because Ignacio told me a lot about you, but it can be summed up pretty simply. He's disappointed in you. He thinks you're worthless and disloyal. He doesn't think you'll ever do anything with your life."

The air stagnated as my accusation hummed through the room.

"Shut the fuck up," he growled, his teeth bared like fangs. "You're lying. He would never tell you any of that."

I shrugged. "Think what you want, but you wouldn't be living in Ryker's home begging for his help if it wasn't true. If you were a real man, you'd take care of your messes instead of forcing your family to do it for you."

I shouldn't have said it. I should've walked away and waited for Ryker in his room, but I couldn't stop myself. Seeing his face—the man who put so much destruction and chaos into motion—ignited something inside of me. I wanted to wound him and tear his life apart even if I could only do it with a few well-placed barbs.

Rever's nose flared, and his dark eyes glowed like polished obsidian. I retreated, taking baby steps backward while eyeing the clenching of his hands.

"I don't know why Ryker tolerates you. It certainly isn't your sparkling personality or welcoming attitude. Maybe you're blackmailing him."

I moved to the other side of the rectangular coffee table, putting something solid between us. "That's ridiculous. How would that work exactly?"

"You're right." He cocked his head to the side. "Ryker would outsmart you. Maybe he's just taking pleasure in fucking you under Evan Deveron's nose. You're the toy he's dangling in front of Evan's face, taunting him. He always had a twisted sense of humor."

"You're an asshole," I yelled and tossed the contents of my bottle of water in his face.

His eyebrows scaled his forehead, and he raised his hands in the air. "What the hell?" He wiped the back of his hand across his lips.

"You started it." I snatched the marble coaster off the coffee table and held it up next to my head, prepared to strike if he came one inch closer to me. "Leave me alone."

Rever shook his head. "I can't believe Ignacio tolerated you in his home for more than a few hours."

"I can't believe he didn't smother you at birth," I countered.

The front door flung open. "What the hell are you two doing?" Ryker said, pausing near the entrance.

My head snapped to the side, then I eyed the coaster in my hand. "Trying to kill each other."

Rever snorted, his shirt and face still dripping with water. I smirked, and a laugh bubbled out of my mouth. We looked ridiculous. We were ridiculous.

"She started it," Rever said, a wide smile on his face as he pointed his finger at me.

I folded my arms across my chest and tapped my foot on the hardwood floors. "I did not."

Ryker rolled his shoulders back and knitted his brows. "Rever, I told you to stay away from her."

Rever held up his hands. "Don't be mad at me. She's the one who took off to do God knows what the minute you walked out the door."

"She's not a prisoner." Ryker's eyes flickered to me as he shrugged out of his black leather jacket. "But a note or call would be nice, Hattie."

Blood heated my face. "I'm sorry. My mom wanted to meet."

"Rever, can you leave us alone for a few minutes?"

"My pleasure," Rever said, practically running out of the room.

When the door to Rever's room closed, Ryker sat in the gray lounge chair. "What happened with Rever?"

I chewed on the inside of my cheek for a second. "Nothing really," I finally answered. "We were tossing insults at each other."

He cocked an eyebrow. "And water?"

My lips twitched. "Yeah, that too."

He nodded. "What did your mom want?"

My eyes darted around the room, landing everywhere but on him. "Don't worry. I took care of it."

"No more secrets, remember?"

I drifted forward and sat on the arm of his chair. "I know."

"Then, tell me what you're hiding," he said as he pulled me into his lap.

I stared at him for a second, deciding what information I wanted to reveal. "She wants me to go on a weekend getaway with my family and Evan's family next weekend."

His arms tensed around my waist. "What'd you say?"

"Do you even have to ask?" I flicked his chest. "Of course I didn't agree. Evan fed my dad a pile of psychobabble bullshit and now she's freaking out."

Ryker tipped up my chin. "About what?"

"That I'm suffering from Stockholm syndrome and that's why I rejected him. I think they planned some sort of intervention during the vacation."

He tensed, and shadows flashed through his eyes. "Do you think that's a fair assessment?"

We sat awkwardly, staring at each other, words singeing the tips of our tongues. I had so many answers to his question, but I feared breaking our truce. Finally, he nodded. "You do."

I shifted, and my legs straddled his waist. "I can't deny the thought has crossed my mind. More frequently in Mexico than recently."

He winced, then lifted me off his body, placing me on the armrest again. Wordlessly, he stood and crossed the room.

"Where are you going?"

"Nowhere." He pointed to a white bag next to the door. "I bought you some clothes if you plan to stick around for a few days."

I cocked my head to the side. "If I plan to stay?"

"It's up to you." He stuffed his hands into his pockets.

I took a few cautious steps closer to him and placed my open palm against his chest. "You're mad."

"No." He grimaced as he shook his head slowly from side to side.

"We promised not to lie or keep secrets."

He blew out a breath. "I'm not asking you to lie

to me about how you feel."

"Then, what?" I asked, searching his face.

"I don't know, Hattie." He backed away from me, and my hand slipped from his chest. "I have some stuff to do. I'll be back in a couple hours." He cracked open the door. "There's food in the refrigerator for dinner."

"What the hell is wrong? What did I do?"

He glared at me, his veins vibrating in his neck. "I'll tell you what's wrong with me. I'm sick of the back and forth."

His harsh tone slashed at my heart. "Back and forth?" The anger radiating from him prompted me to take a step back. We eyed each other, sizing each other up like two boxers in a ring.

"You know exactly what I'm talking about. One minute you want this, and the next you're running away. Pushing me away. Throwing every roadblock you can come up with in my face."

"Ryker." I held out my hand to him. "It's complicated."

His hand sliced through the air and darkness swirled in eyes. "Fucking save it. I don't want to talk about it right now."

"Why are you leaving? We need to talk."

"We've talked, but you're still riding the fence while I'm all in. I picked you over my family, and you still can't decide how you feel about me. You're in. You're out. You have Stockholm syndrome. Well, you know what? I'm sick of it."

"You can't blame me. In Mexico, you put out a million mixed signals, and then you pushed me away—"

184

"Mexico." He yanked on the roots of his hair. "Fuck what happened in Mexico. I had a job to do, and I was conflicted as fuck. I wanted you even when I knew I shouldn't touch you."

"Why?"

"Because regardless of what happened between us, I knew how it ended."

"And how was it supposed to end?"

"Exactly the way it did. With you running back to Evan. Tell me. How long did it take for him to convince you to marry him? A day? An hour? Ten minutes?"

"How dare you," I screamed. "I did what you asked and now you're pissed. If you wanted me, you shouldn't have let me go. You shouldn't have thrown me at Evan with your blessing."

"I had to let you go."

"No you didn't," I protested, whipping my head back and forth. "You could've asked me to stay. You could've fought for me. You didn't do any of that."

His mouth twisted into a sneer and he pointed his finger at me. "Are you trying to tell me you would've given up everything to stay with me? Your family? Your friends? Finishing your degree? You would've been happy disappearing forever? Because that's what we would've had to do."

My shoulders sagged as the anger drained from my body. I wanted to wrap my arms around him and tell him I loved him, but I held back. "No, you're right, but things are different now. I choose you. I chose you. I'm just confused. I'm not sure how to navigate everything." I was more than confused. I was driving blind, in a blizzard at night on an unlit road without GPS.

"You say that now, but the next time something happens you don't like, you'll run again, expecting me to chase you and convince you to change your mind."

"That's not true." I reached for him, but he held up his hands, putting a symbolic wall between us. We didn't need any more walls. We had too many already.

"I'll be back later. If you're still here, we'll talk." He shut the door before a response filtered through my brain.

I leaned my head against the door and closed my eyes. "I'll be here," I whispered.

Chapter Twenty

Ryker

I did everything I could think of to avoid going home and facing Hattie. Fuck, I didn't even know if she'd be there when I went back. I didn't make much of an argument for her to stay. I practically shoved her out of my life.

I drove in endless loops around the city. I stopped for dinner at my favorite burger joint. I went to a bar around the corner from my condo building and drank too many drinks to drive home safely.

I called Ignacio. He didn't answer. I didn't know what I would've said to him anyway. We talked on an as-needed basis, which translated into once a month. Granted, we had talked more frequently since Rever became my temporary roommate. Rever didn't think Ignacio knew where he was, but as usual, Rever underestimated our dad. Ignacio knew everything. I wouldn't be surprised if he knew about Anna's pregnancy, or Rever's freelance drug smuggling.

Around ten o'clock, I called my mom. I hadn't talked to her in months. When she found out I planned to help Ignacio get Rever out of prison, we had a huge fight. Until tonight, neither of us had tried to mend our relationship. Both of us were too stubborn for our own good.

"Mom, it's Ryker."

"I know who it is. You're the only person who'd call me at this time of the night."

I chuckled. "It's not that late."

"Do you know how old I am? I need at least eight hours of sleep or I'll have bags under my eyes the size of Rhode Island."

"You're exaggerating. You're the most beautiful fifty-five-year-old woman I've ever seen." It was true. She'd modeled in her late teens and early twenties.

"Your compliment lost some momentum when you qualified it with my age," she grumbled, but I could hear the smile in her voice. For a former model, she didn't have a vain bone in her body. Unlike some women who did anything to hang onto their youth, my mom embraced her age. She exercised, she ate healthily, but she didn't do anything too drastic to remedy the lines around her eyes or erase the gray from her hair.

"You're right."

"I'm always right."

I sighed, knowing what I needed to do. "I'm sorry, Mom."

"Sorry for what?"

"For fighting with you."

The silence stretched, and for a second, I didn't

know if she'd accept my apology. "You don't need to apologize. We can agree to disagree, but it doesn't change how much I love you. How's your brother? Did everything go well?"

"I'm still working on it."

"I read that he was released from jail."

"He was, but there have been a few complications."

She snorted. "I wouldn't have expected anything less."

"Mom," I cautioned.

"I know. I know," she said wearily. "But you have to realize how this is going to end."

"What do you mean?"

"Ignacio wants you under his thumb. He'll have you waist deep in cartel business before you know it, and then you'll be stuck."

"That's not going to happen."

She sighed. "Then you don't know Ignacio very well. He thinks the Vargas Cartel is his legacy, his crowning achievement, and now he knows Rever is incapable of leading the cartel into the next generation. That leaves you."

"No. I've already told him I can't help him."

She exhaled loudly. "If you don't sever all contact with him, he will find a way to rope you into his depraved way of life."

"Mom," I said, dragging out the word. "We've had this conversation before."

"And this won't be the last time. I'll keep saying it until it's too late, or you've kicked your father out of your life for good." She cleared her throat. "Why are you calling?"

"To talk."

"Are you sure that's it?"

I slid my hands up and down my legs. "I've met someone. A woman."

"Do you love her?"

I nodded, even though she couldn't see me. "I do." It felt strange confessing this to my mom before telling Hattie. My mom and I were never close. I loved her. She loved me. She'd been a good mom, but an invisible wall existed between us. For as long as I could remember, my mom and dad communicated through intermediaries. The deep fracture between my mom and dad made me feel constantly divided. Divided between two parents, two lives, two countries, and two cultures. Any love I showed my dad felt like a betrayal of my mom and vice versa, so I existed in limbo, never fully pledging myself to anyone or anything.

"You haven't told her anything about your family or your job." It was a statement, not a question.

"She knows everything."

"Really?" she said, sounding surprised. "How'd she take it?"

I paused, not sure how to answer her question. There wasn't a simple answer, and I refused to reveal the details of how we met. My mom would never forgive me. She'd lose all faith in me. "She doesn't like it."

"Does she still want to be with you?"

Pain knifed through my gut. I felt like I'd been punched in the stomach, and I couldn't catch my breath. "I hope so."

"You don't know?"

"It's complicated," I countered, reciting the same words Hattie said to me earlier. The irony of my declaration didn't go unnoticed by me.

"Love always is," she whispered, sounding tired.

"I'll let you get back to sleep."

"Okay, but don't wait another two months to call me."

I laughed. "You can call me too, Mom."

"I know. Goodnight, Ryker."

"Goodnight, Mom."

***

Two hours later, my hand rested on the door handle to my bedroom. A cold feeling prickled through my body, and my heart plummeted to my stomach. I didn't know what I'd do if Hattie had left me. After four glasses of bourbon, I had promised I'd let her go if that was what she wanted. I didn't want her to be mine by default, or because she felt some perverse attachment to me.

Now, with the moment of truth staring right back at me, my chest burned with the thought of never seeing her, touching her, or kissing her again. Somehow over the last few months, she had become more important to me than anything or anyone else in the world. I ached to pull her into my arms and lose myself in the taste of her lips.

Closing my eyes, I pushed my bedroom door open and sucked in a deep breath before I faced reality. Relief flooded through my veins when I saw her curled in a ball on my bed. She wore my gray

191

collared shirt. Her long, toned legs were twisted in the sheets like she had a hard time falling asleep. She looked like a fallen angel with hair framing her face and the fringe of her dark lashes shadowing her cheeks.

Not wanting to wake her, I moved through the room as silently as possible. I placed a small plastic bag on the nightstand and trailed my fingers down the side of her face. She didn't move. With my eyes locked on her face, I pulled my shirt over my head, kicked off my shoes, and shoved my pants down my legs.

Sitting down next to her, I traced the curve of her face and the arch of her long neck, committing it to memory for the thousandth time. Her eyes fluttered open.

"Ryker?" she whispered, her voice raspy from sleep. "What time is it?"

"After midnight."

"I tried to wait up for you. Do you want me to leave? Is that why you didn't come back for dinner?"

Her words tore at my heart, slashing invisible ribbons across the planes of my chest. "I'm sorry," I whispered hoarsely, remorse suffocating me. My hands skated up and down her arms. "I'm so sorry. I don't want you to go."

"I'm sorry too." She rested the palm of her smooth hand on my cheek, and a shudder raced through my body. "I didn't mean what I said. I know this situation is hard for both of us. I didn't mean to dismiss my feelings for you."

"Shh." I placed a finger over her lips, rubbing it

back and forth. "Don't apologize. I don't want your apology."

Two deep grooves marred the smooth skin at the bridge of her nose. "You don't?"

"No." I kissed her, lingering on her lips for a beat too long, tasting her and inhaling her familiar scent. "You're the only one who doesn't need to apologize for what's happened. You haven't done anything wrong. You've been pushed and pulled in every direction. You're doing the best you can. You have every right to be confused and question me. Us. Everything. I won't push you again. Any time you want out or you feel like this is too hard, you can go."

Her hands sunk in my hair, and she pulled my mouth back against hers. I parted her lips and groaned as her tongue curled around mine with an unyielding urgency. She turned her head to the side, severing contact. Her golden eyes seared mine. I couldn't breathe. I couldn't look away as my heartbeat reverberated through my body, waiting for her to say something. Anything.

"I love you," she whispered.

The air whooshed out of my lungs. With those three simple words, she had healed the division in my heart, mending the fractured pieces. I didn't need to choose one-half of my heart over the other. She owned the whole damn thing.

My loyalties weren't divided.

My heart wasn't conflicted.

My soul wasn't fractured.

She owned every inch of me, whether she wanted it or not.

Chapter Twenty-One

Hattie

Ryker froze. His eyes widened, and his hands tightened on my arms. For a split second, I wished I could rewind time and recall my words. With every passing second of silence, my heart died a little. When I couldn't take one more second of his silent condemnation, I closed my eyes, drowning in dark tidal waves of self-pity and self-censure.

"Open your eyes, Hattie."

I shook my head. "No. I'm sorry I said it. I should've kept it to myself. We can pretend like it didn't happen."

"I can't do that," he said, resting his forehead against mine.

I rolled my head to the side. "Please," I whispered.

He cradled my face, gently forcing me to face him. I didn't open my eyes, but I felt his nose brush against mine.

"I love you too."

My eyes popped open as my heart did a victory

dance in my chest. "You do?"

He grunted in disbelief and frustration. "Of course I do."

"I never thought…I didn't know," I murmured more to myself than him.

"Now you do." Our lips fused together in a frenzy of desire like this was the first time we had ever kissed.

Our mouths tangled.

Our hearts united.

Our bodies harmonized.

Our breathing quickened.

I loved him. Every flaw. Every secret. Every smile. Every inch of him. Nothing could change my mind. I could've carved out my heart and given it to him right then because he owned it. Every jigsaw piece belonged irrevocably to Ryker Vargas.

My lover.

My captor.

My other half.

My future.

Button by button, he opened my shirt, taking his time like I was the best present he'd ever received. Then, he slid my panties down my legs. His boxer briefs followed. Skin to skin, I ached to feel him inside of me again. I didn't want to waste one more second. I reached between our bodies to guide him inside of me, but he snagged my wrists one by one and pressed them against the headboard.

Ryker had other ideas. "Not so fast," he muttered.

He trailed kisses along my jaw, down my neck, and then licked a path to the delicate skin behind my ear. Each flicker of his tongue sent a rush of pleasure through my body. He kneaded my breasts, soft and gentle, and circled my nipples with his thumbs. Then, his mouth followed his talented fingers, and I was lost. Moaning, I arched into him, offering and begging for him to take anything he wanted.

One of his hands slipped down my body to my sex. I spread my legs, intentionally giving him better access. His finger swirled around my entrance, then he stroked in and out of me with two fingers. My hips rotated as he moved with the hands of a man who knew how to play my body, igniting every nerve ending. He always had. He always would.

"Ryker," I gasped, so close to the edge my vision blurred. The ache inside of me multiplied with startling velocity, becoming hotter and more urgent with each thrust of his fingers.

"What do you want, Hattie?"

"You. Inside. Me. Now." I wanted to experience the soul-shattering connection when he buried himself deep inside of me, and we moved together like we were meant for each other.

His eyes darkened with promise, and his hand stopped moving. "Now?" he whispered, his lips hovering inches from mine.

"Yes," I answered, because there was no reason to fight him anymore. No reason to pretend. We were on the same page. We were moving forward together. No secrets. No lies. Only love.

He moved his hand and shifted his body so his hard cock rested against my sex. He flexed his hips, tormenting me with the slow slide of his cock along my entrance until I thought I'd die of emptiness. With his eyes searing mine, he slid inside of me, filling me, stretching me. As he began to move, everything faded but the feel of him inside of me and the warm brush of his lips against mine.

Perfection.

Completion.

Beauty.

Those three words tumbled through my mind as he glided in and out of me with long, languid strokes—each rock, tilt, and flex bringing me closer and closer to completion. I groaned, voicing my need the only way I could at that moment.

"Does that feel good?" I nodded almost too eagerly, and a suggestion of a smile tugged at the corner of his lips. "I know. We're perfect together."

He was right. Maybe that was why I could never refuse him. I circled my legs around his waist and tilted my hips as he moved with the perfect carnal rhythm, igniting a slow burn in every nerve ending. He consumed me with every touch, kiss, and thrust.

In moments like this, only Ryker and I existed. His room could burst into flames, and I wouldn't care or notice. His hand moved to the apex of my thighs. One masterfully aimed touch and the slow burn exploded into a wildfire. I cried out as an orgasm ripped through my body. He moved faster, harder, wringing every ounce of pleasure from my body and his until he collapsed on top of me, the strong and heavy beat of his heart nudging my breastbone.

With his head buried next to my neck, his thumb

traced the edge of my jaw. "I love you," he whispered. I turned my head and pressed a sideways kiss on the center of his palm.

"I love you too."

He rolled off me and chuckled.

"What's so funny?" I stared at his smiling face.

"Nothing. I'm happy."

"Me too," I said, and I was. For the first time in months, I believed everything would be fine. Better than fine. Ryker made me believe in us, in him, and our future. Regardless of what happened with my family or Evan's family, I had Ryker, and at that moment, nothing else mattered. "Having you in my life makes me happy."

His mouth found mine, kissing me, loving me, and telling me without words everything I needed to know.

Chapter Twenty-Two

Ryker

I placed a tray on the bed next to Hattie. I could get used to waking up next to her every day. She looked so peaceful with her dark hair spread out on my sheets. The morning sunlight flooded the bedroom, highlighting the contours of her body.

I had never wanted the women I dated in my space, touching my belongings and demanding my attention the morning after, but Hattie made me want that and more.

When she left Mexico, I thought I'd be able to forget about her, but it never happened. Days passed, weeks passed, and I craved her more and more. She complicated my life from the minute I saw her, and now I couldn't imagine my life without her.

Last night, we finally talked about what we meant to each other. We loved each other, but so many obstacles stood in our way. I planned to fight for a life with her even though I didn't know what it'd look like, because being with her felt...right.

I stroked the side of her face and her eyes fluttered open. "Good morning."

"Hey," she whispered. "What's that?" She sat up, eyeing the tray of food.

"Breakfast in bed."

She smiled. "Really?"

"Yes. Don't look surprised. I can be a good guy when I want to be."

She balanced the tray on her legs and cocked her head to the side. "You know what—I think you're on to something. You're not so bad when your moods aren't all over the place."

I kissed her. I didn't have a choice. I had to wipe that sassy smile off her face. "Watch out."

"Or what?" she mumbled against my lips.

"Or I'll spend the rest of the day punishing you."

"Hm." She leaned against the headboard. "That sounds promising, but let me enjoy my food first. Then you can get to work summoning your inner asshole."

Chuckling, I averted my gaze. Out of the corner of my eye, I saw the plastic bag I'd left on the nightstand last night. My mood dropped instantly. I didn't want to ruin her morning, but we couldn't avoid reality forever.

"Ryker," she said as she squeezed my hand. "You know I was kidding, right?"

"Yeah." With a forced smile, I grabbed the plastic bag and sat down on the edge of the bed.

Hattie took a sip of her coffee. "What's that?"

I slipped the box out of the bag and placed it on the tray.

Her lip pressed into a firm line. "A pregnancy

test? I already took one a couple weeks ago, remember?"

I swallowed and shifted on the bed. "I know, but I think you should try again. Just to be sure."

"I feel fine." She picked up the box and squinted at the small text on the back. "I'm not nauseous, tired, or whatever."

"That's good."

She held out the box to me. "Save it for me, and if I still haven't started my period in a week, I'll take the test."

I grabbed it out of her hand. "You're procrastinating."

Ignoring me, she took a few bites of her toast. "I took a test already."

"I know, but you may have taken it too early."

She frowned. "How do you figure?"

"You'd only been home for two weeks. That's fourteen days."

"I know how long two weeks is," she muttered.

I held out the box. "Right, so you agree it might've been too early to take the test."

She tugged on the hem of her shirt. "I'm not ready to know. I'm still trying to put my life back together."

"Negative or positive, it won't change anything." I placed the box in her lap.

"You're wrong." She swallowed hard. "It will change everything. What would I do with a baby? I haven't finished school. I don't have a job anymore. My family barely talks to me. They think I'm crazy. I'm living off my savings and the money my dad deposits in my bank account every month to assuage his guilt for being a shitty parent." She rubbed her hand over her face. "I'm a fucking mess."

I moved the tray from her lap and wrapped my arms around her. "No, you're not, and you have me. I already told you. We're in this together."

"And you won't be mad if I am..." Her voice lowered until it faded away entirely. Tears bloomed in the corners of her eyes. She looked fragile, like she'd shatter any second. Her eyes were haunted; her golden skin stretched tight over the delicate bones of her face.

"No," I answered before she could finish the thought.

I hadn't planned to have a family, but I wouldn't be mad. I'd spent my life being my dad's dirty secret and my mom's life changing mistake. My dad already had a wife and a kid. My mom's modeling career crashed and burned after she had me. Both of them loved me in their own way, but I always suspected they believed they'd be better off without me. I didn't want my child to feel that way. If Hattie were pregnant, I'd make damn sure she and my child were happy and had everything they needed.

"Are you sure? Because even if I'm pregnant, I could—"

I pressed my fingers to her lips. "We're not having this discussion."

She yanked my fingers away from her face. "What do you mean?"

"After you've taken the test, and we know for sure, we'll talk and we'll decide what we want to do together."

"Okay." She picked up the box from her lap and tapped it against her leg. "Let's do this."

I stood up and grabbed her hand, pulling her to her feet. We walked to the bathroom, with our hands intertwined.

She stopped outside the door. "You can wait out here. I don't need your help to pee on a stick."

"Whatever you need."

When she closed the door, I slid down the wall and pulled my phone out of my pocket. It had been vibrating in my pocket all morning. I'd successfully ignored all the calls, but someone really wanted to get in touch with me.

I scrolled through my missed calls. All ten of them were from Ignacio. I hesitated for a moment. Then, I snuck away to the bedroom and called him back. I only had a few minutes, but maybe that'd be enough time to figure out what he wanted.

"Is this Ryker?"

"Yes," I answered, not recognizing the voice.

"This is Emanuel Rodriquez. I don't think we've met, but I work for you dad."

"I know who you are." Ignacio hadn't introduced us, but he mentioned him often. Sometimes I wondered why he didn't groom Emanuel to be his successor instead of Rever. Emanuel was dedicated to the Vargas Cartel like Rever and I would never be. He didn't have a problem dealing with the ugly side of the business.

"I tried to call Rever last night, but he hasn't answered his phone."

"If you called from Ignacio's phone, he won't

answer. They aren't speaking."

"Right," he said. "I forgot."

"Can I help you with something?"

He sighed. "I don't know how to tell you this, so I'll just come out and say it. Ignacio was shot last night."

My vision blurred, and my breath stagnated in my throat. "What? How?"

"I don't know the details, but from what little I've been told by his security team, it sounded like a paid hit."

My throat closed and I clutched my phone harder. Ignacio and I weren't always on the best of terms. He was a hard and sometimes unforgiving man, but he was my dad, and I loved him. "Is he going to be okay?" My voice cracked.

"He's in the intensive care unit. He was shot in the chest. He has a collapsed lung, and he's lost a lot of blood."

"Fuck," I mumbled in a daze. "What does the doctor think?"

"He made it through surgery and they were able to repair his lung. They're going to take him off the ventilator tomorrow. We'll know more then."

I tunneled my hands in my hair. "Okay. Thanks for calling."

Emanuel didn't respond for a moment and the phone crackled with silence. "I think you and Rever should come, just in case..." He didn't finish the sentence, but I understood what he meant. Ignacio wasn't a young man, and even if he were, recovering from a gunshot wound wasn't a sure thing.

"I have to make some arrangements, but we'll be there as soon as possible." Details tumbled through my mind. I didn't think Rever could get on a commercial flight without being arrested. I could try to get him a counterfeit passport from one of my contacts, but it'd take a couple of days. "Maybe three days," I clarified.

He cleared his throat. "Ignacio's private jet arrived at Ronald Regan International Airport an hour ago. It can leave as soon as you're ready."

I never liked using Ignacio's plane or taking his money. It always came with strings a mile long, but it'd simplify things. "Thanks. Text me the hospital information. Rever and I will go straight there after we land."

"See you tonight."

I disconnected the phone and braced my head on my knees.

Chapter Twenty-Three

Hattie

With my back facing the stick slated to determine my future, I tapped my fingers against my thighs, mentally counting off the minutes in sixty-second increments. Counting helped me ignore all the questions circling in my brain with ruthless determination.

Fifty-eight.

Fifty-nine.

Sixty.

This was it—the moment of truth.

I rubbed my eyes, sucked in a breath, and spun around. Leaning over, I stared at the white thermometer-like stick, careful not to disturb anything.

Two lines. There were two fucking lines. With trembling hands, I snagged the crumbled instructions off the counter, making sure I didn't misinterpret them. Nope.

"Oh my God," I whispered. "I'm pregnant."

What would I tell my family? My mom would

freak. She dropped out of Harvard Law School when she found out she was pregnant with my brother. She referred to it as the dumbest mistake of her life, and here I was, pregnant, unmarried, and months away from receiving my graduate degree.

I'm screwed.

My vision tilted like I had vertigo, and my knees buckled like an accordion. I clenched the edge of the countertop, barely catching myself before I collapsed. Tears welded in the corners of my eyes, threatening to erupt like a volcano.

What would I do? I paced back and forth with my hand cradling my still flat stomach for endless minutes. Distantly, I wondered why Ryker hadn't knocked on the door yet. Pausing, I stared at my reflection in the mirror.

I can do this. I'm smart. I can figure this out.

Ryker would help me with whatever I decided. I trusted him. I splashed some water on my face, picked up the white stick, and cracked the door.

"Ryker," I said, poking my head out. I didn't see him. I walked into his bedroom, searching everywhere for him.

"Ryker," I said again.

Five seconds later, he walked out of his closet and dumped a black hard-shelled suitcase on the bed. He didn't look at me. He didn't acknowledge me. Instead, he unzipped the suitcase and flipped it open.

"I'm pregnant," I blurted out before I lost my nerve.

He didn't respond. He opened the dresser behind him and pulled out a stack of clothes.

My stomach dropped. "Did you hear me?"

He paused mid-stride. His eyes locked with mine. His face was pale and his eyes were red-rimmed, but he smiled. "No. I'm sorry. I was lost in my thoughts. What did you find out?"

I waved my hand at the opened luggage. "Are you going somewhere?"

Sighing, he dropped the clothes on the bed. "To Mexico."

"Why?" I held out the pregnancy test and wrapped my other hand around my waist.

He eyed the white stick, then he grabbed it out of my hand. "Ignacio is in the hospital."

"What happened?"

"Somebody shot him last night." He twirled the stick between his fingers. Then, he lifted his head. "You're pregnant?"

My mouth opened and closed. I didn't know what to say. Nothing seemed right. Not now. I nodded. "Yes," I whispered, closing my eyes. "I'm sorry. This is a mess. What do you want me to do?"

His arms closed around my waist, and he wrenched me against his chest. His hand ran up and down the back of my hair. He didn't say anything as we swayed back and forth. After a few minutes, he turned my face, forcing me to look at him. "You're going to come with me."

"To Mexico?"

"Yes. We're leaving in a couple of hours. We'll stop by Vera's apartment on the way to the airport. You can grab your passport and pack a bag, but we don't have much time."

Fear ripped through me and my throat

constricted. My shuddering breath echoed off the barren walls. "I can't." I jerked my head back and forth. "I want to be there for you, but I don't want to go back there ever again. I don't want to see Ignacio. I don't want to stay at his house." I didn't need to explain. I didn't owe him any explanation. He would understand.

"I know, Hattie, but I can't leave you here. Especially now."

I stepped out of his embrace and laced my hands together in front of my chest, squeezing them until my fingertips turned pink. "I'll be okay. It'll give me time to think. This might actually be a good thing." I didn't really believe that. I wanted him to stay, but I knew he couldn't. Ignacio had committed and ordered innumerable depraved acts, but he was still Ryker's father.

His dark eyebrows drew together. "Where will you stay? You can't go back to Vera's apartment yet."

My gaze drifted over his room, desperately searching for a compromise. I didn't want to go back to Vera's apartment. I still couldn't ignore that she might've helped Evan, even if it was only in a limited capacity. Also, I wasn't ready to tell anyone about the pregnancy. In a matter of days, I could experience morning sickness, and she only had one bathroom. The stomach flu excuse would only work for a few days.

"I'll stay here. I'll get some of my things." When he didn't respond, I realized he might not want me in his apartment by myself. "If that's okay with you. I'd stay out of your personal space. You can keep your study locked or whatever. I won't tell anyone I'm here," I rambled.

"No," he answered, not even taking a second to consider my suggestion.

"You don't trust me?" Confusion and sadness swirled around me.

He folded his arms across his chest. "I trust you, but I'm not leaving you here to figure out everything by yourself. We need to talk, but I don't have time to do it right now. I have a plane to catch. I have to tell Rever what's going on."

"Did you buy me a plane ticket?"

He shook his head. "We're not flying commercial."

"I don't know," I whispered. "I'm not sure it's a good idea."

"Look, you don't have to see Ignacio or anyone affiliated with the Vargas Cartel. We'll stay at a hotel in a touristy area. I won't take you anywhere near the Vargas compound. You can hang out at the pool while I'm gone. Think of it as a vacation. You won't have to deal with your family or Evan. We'll work out the details of your pregnancy."

My stomach knotted at the thought of facing my mom or running into Evan, but more importantly, my heart begged me to go with him. To trust him. "I could work on my thesis for school," I said, pushing my forebodings aside.

Striding forward with a smile on his face, he cradled my face and kissed me on the lips hard. "Good. We'll stop by Vera's on the way to the airport, and you can grab your laptop and whatever else you need."

"How long will we be gone?"

"A week. Maybe two, but you can leave anytime you want."

I searched his face for duplicity, but he looked sincere. "You promise?"

"Yes." He kissed me again. "Anything you want. I need to see Ignacio, but you're my first priority."

Chapter Twenty~Four

Ryker

We landed in Cancun at ten o'clock last night. Hospital visiting hours had ended, so Hattie and I took a cab to the hotel instead. I didn't know where Rever went, and I didn't care. Even though he said he didn't want to see Ignacio, I assumed I'd see him at the hospital sometime today.

"What are you going to do today?" I asked Hattie.

We hadn't exchanged more than a few sentences on the plane or last night. It didn't appear the trend would reverse course this morning either. We dressed. We walked to the hotel restaurant for breakfast. We ordered food. We sipped our coffee and ate, but we had only said a handful of words to each other.

Every unspoken word and missed opportunity to reassure her pressed against my chest, suffocating me. Anxiety leached from her pores. Her hands shook every time she lifted her fork. Her eye twitched. She was nervous about being in Mexico with me again. I understood her concerns. I hated being here again too. The ghosts from the last time we were in Mexico haunted me. I wished I could erase all her pain and sadness with happier memories.

Hattie set her silverware diagonally across her plate and pushed the plate away from her. She hardly touched her food. "I'll do some research and try to work on my thesis, or maybe I'll lounge by the pool. Swim some laps. I haven't thought about it."

"You can come with me," I offered. "You don't have to go in his room or anything. You could wait in the lounge area. We could go out to lunch."

Her eyes locked on mine for a second, then they flickered away. "I don't think that's a good idea."

"I don't like the idea of you sitting at the hotel by yourself."

She smiled, but it didn't reach her eyes. "I'll be fine. I have plenty of things to occupy my time. Don't worry about me."

I frowned. "Of course I'm going to worry about you. You're pregnant and—"

She held up her hand as she chewed the corner of her lower lip. "P-pl-please," she stuttered, struggling to force the word from her throat. "Not right now. Not when you're leaving me here alone for the rest of the day. Not when I won't have anything to distract me from analyzing every word you said. Every word I said."

"Hattie," I said, lowering my voice.

"No." She moved her head from side to side. "Later, okay?"

I wanted to grab her arm, pull her against my body, and kiss her until she understood how much I loved her—how much I wanted to pack our bags and get on the first plane back to the States. I didn't do any of those things.

"Tonight?"

"Sure." She ran her fingers along my jaw. "What time do you think you'll be back?"

"I'm not sure, but I'll try to make it back here before dinner." My cell phone rang. It was Emanuel. I didn't want to take the call in front of Hattie. "I have to go." I pressed a kiss to the corner of her mouth and stood up.

"I'm sorry I've been so quiet. I'm just…" She cleared her throat and averted her eyes.

"Nervous about being in Mexico again," I said, finishing her sentence.

She swallowed. "Yeah, but I don't want you to think I'm mad at you, because I'm not."

"I know. I get it. I know this trip is uncomfortable, but it means a lot to me that you came."

"Thanks for understanding." She squeezed my hand. "Call me and tell me what's going on."

"I will."

***

I sat in a chair next to my dad's hospital bed. The smell of medicine and antiseptic filled my lungs. He looked smaller and older than I remembered. His skin was ashen, and his cheeks were sunken. He had a black eye and scratches on the side of his face.

214

According to Emanuel, the doctors successfully removed the ventilator earlier this morning, but he still had a chest tube to help his lungs function and remove any residual fluids from his chest cavity.

"How are you feeling?" I asked.

"About as good as I look," Ignacio croaked.

"So you feel like shit?"

His lips twitched. "*Exactamente.*" He closed his bloodshot, filmy eyes. "Where's Rever?"

"I don't know. He said he'd be here."

"Hm," he muttered without opening his eyes.

I reached out and grasped his hand. "I'm glad you're going to be okay."

"That remains to be seen."

"You're not out of the woods, but you're breathing on your own. That's a good sign."

He opened his eyes. "I heard you brought Hattie with you. Is she in the waiting room, or did you leave her at the hotel?"

I dropped his hand and rested my elbows on my knees. "She's at the hotel."

"I figured as much. I can't imagine she wants to see me." He lifted his arm and winced.

"She's busy writing her thesis," I said, ignoring his comment. Hattie didn't want to see him, and I couldn't blame her.

"How are things with her?"

"It's a mess. Senator Deveron linked my two identities and not a day goes by without another threat." After the confrontation in the alley with his goons, Senator Deveron hadn't backed down. In fact, his threats had escalated. Some of the shit he said about Hattie and my family turned my stomach. I wanted to meet him in a dark alley and beat the shit out of him.

"Are you worried?"

I rubbed my jaw, carefully considering my answer. "I have enough dirt on him to make him think twice about acting on any of his threats, but…"

"But what?" he prompted.

"I'm worried about your arrangement with him."

"Don't."

"What do you mean?"

"Don't worry about me. Do what you need to do. You and Rever are good at that."

I nodded as I studied his face. "Do you know he made threats against the Vargas Cartel and you? He said he'd back the Alvarez Cartel."

Ignacio breathed hard through his nose as his ebony eyes collided with mine. "Have you changed your mind about taking your place with the Vargas Cartel?"

"No."

"Great, then why the fuck do you care?"

"Are you saying I shouldn't care?"

Ignacio groaned. "Why are you here?"

"I'm here because you're my father and I care about you. Isn't that a good enough reason?"

"No. I have nurses to sit at my bedside and change my bedpan. I need help with the family business. I need someone to watch over my interests while I'm in here."

"I can't do that. I don't want any part of that life."

"Obviously, I can't count on either of my sons."

He shook his head. "Just go. I don't want you here right now."

I pushed out of my chair. "So it's all or nothing? What happened to your speeches about doing what I needed to do?"

His lips twisted, and the angles of his face stood out in sharp relief like they were carved from the cruelty and violence he doled out without a trace of conscience. "I changed my mind. I don't have the luxury of having people in my life with divided loyalties. If my sons don't respect me, nobody will. I'm tired of this game. I'm tired of waiting for you to realize your place. You don't respect me. You aren't loyal."

My hands balled into fists. My fingers itched to grab him by the collar of his hospital gown and shake him. I'd given up so much and done so many regrettable things, but it'd never be enough for him. Every time he needed help, I was there. It was pointless to keep living like this, never belonging anywhere or with anyone. Fuck him and his cartel. "I think it's time for me to leave."

"I think you're right," he said, his eyes deadly calm. "Don't contact me until you're ready to assume your legacy."

My nostrils flared as poisonous words dangled from the tip of my tongue, but I didn't say any of them. Instead, I walked out of the room and out of his life without looking back, removing myself from my father's venomous glare and toxic life. My muscles tensed with regret, my head throbbed with the realization of how much time I wasted on my father, but my mind was clearer than it'd been in years. He liberated me from guilt and family pressure. I wished he'd done it earlier. I wasted too much of my life trying to please him.

"Don't bother," I spat as I passed Rever in the corridor next to the elevator. I slapped the palm of my hand against the elevator call button.

"What do you mean?" he asked, following me into the elevator.

The doors slid closed, and my wavy reflection in the satin metal taunted me. "You were right," I barked as I stared at floor numbers, a symbolic countdown until I could walk out of the hospital and Ignacio's life forever.

A wide Cheshire grin crept across Rever's face, swallowing his features. "I'm glad you finally realized it, but what are you talking about?"

"Ignacio."

Rever chuckled. "Ah. He gave you an ultimatum. He never lets a crisis go to waste." The elevator doors opened, and I stepped into the lobby without answering.

"See you later." With my back turned to his, I lifted my hand in dismissal and started walking.

"Wait. I came to find you, not to see Ignacio. I don't have any intention of visiting him. I already told you that."

I pushed open the door to freedom. I squinted and slipped on my dark aviator sunglasses. The morning light was intense and harsh after the yellowed light in the hospital.

Ignacio thought he gave me an ultimatum, but he didn't. He gave me freedom. Freedom to be with Hattie. Freedom to walk away from him forever.

Freedom to never look back.

"Why?"

"We need to talk."

I wheeled around to face him. He looked better than he had in weeks. Good for him. He wore a white collared shirt and tan linen pants. He had shaved his face and the circles under his eyes had faded.

"Start talking. I don't have much time."

His dark eyebrows slanted downward into a thick line. "Why not?"

"I'm done here. I'm flying home."

He looked down and tapped the tips of his fingers together. "You can't leave until you help me with Anna. We agreed."

I shrugged. "I changed my mind."

"Just give me one more day. Everything is set for tomorrow. I have the money. Anna will be at church. Emilio will fly us from the Vargas compound to Isla Mujeres and back. I booked a flight to Panama for Anna and me."

I stuffed my hands into my pockets. "What's in it for me? You're paying Emilio, but what are you going to do for me? Why should I risk anything for you?"

He raised his hands in supplication. "We're brothers. That's what brothers do for each other."

I stormed forward. My eyes stung with memories best left in the past. "You've never lifted a finger for me or said one word in my defense. Try again."

Shadows flashed through his dark eyes. We both knew what I meant. Before his mom decided she was done with Ignacio and moved to a different home, she made my summers in Mexico a living hell. She humiliated me and degraded me, never missing an opportunity to remind me I didn't belong. But no matter how Ignacio's wife may have schemed to hurt me mentally and physically, it hurt worse that my flesh and blood had allowed it to happen. Ignacio never offered a single word in protest. The selfish bastard was content to let me pay for his sins.

"If I intervened, it would've made it worse. She felt betrayed and dishonored by Ignacio. He had a son with another woman and he shoved you in her face, flaunting his affair."

My head pounded, and I squeezed the bridge of my nose between my fingertips. "I don't care anymore." I didn't. I had stopped caring years ago.

Rever sighed. "I'm sorry. I wish things were different then and now. As a kid, we were pitted against each other, but it shouldn't have been that way. We were on the same side. My mom didn't love Ignacio. She never did, but she hated the whispers behind her back about his unfaithfulness. Ignacio only cared about his legacy and the Vargas Cartel. We should've fought back."

I nodded. "Probably. Good luck tomorrow."

He grabbed my wrist. "Don't leave me hanging. I'll pay you whatever you want."

"I don't want your money."

"What do you want?"

I stared in the distance for a moment without answering. "A debt for a debt. A favor for a favor," I answered, ripping my wrist out of his grasp.

"What's that mean?"

"You'll repay the favor when the time comes, no questions asked."

He studied my face for a few beats. "Fine." He held out his hand, and I shook it, sealing the deal. I'd help him with Anna, and he'd help me when the time came. It never hurt to have a person indebted to you.

Chapter Twenty-Five

Hattie

Dressed in a short ivory-colored robe, I paced back and forth in the darkened hotel room, eyeing the door as if my life depended on it. The romantic dinner I had planned sat mostly untouched on the balcony. I should've eaten more than a few bites of salad and bread. I was hungry, tired, and pregnant, but at the moment I didn't care about any of those things. My head throbbed. My eyes watered. I wanted to go home, even though I didn't know what that meant anymore.

My parents and Vera had blown up my phone all day. Nobody knew where I was. For all intents and purposes, I had disappeared without a trace again. I couldn't answer their calls. I couldn't send them pictures. Nothing about being back in Mexico, only steps from where I was abducted a few months ago, would reassure them. They'd think I'd lost my mind and have me involuntarily committed the minute I stepped foot on U.S. soil. As the minutes turned into hours, I started to agree with that sentiment.

Just when I decided to give up and go to sleep, the door opened. Ryker stood, leaning his shoulder against the doorframe. His sunglasses hung from the collar of his shirt. His shirt was wrinkled, his sleeves rolled to the middle of his forearms. I stopped pacing.

"You're up."

I rested my hands on my hips. "I am."

"Did you eat?" He looked from me to the open balcony door. The ocean breeze had snuffed out the candles hours ago.

"No. Did you eat?" I shot back.

He dragged a hand over the side of his face. "Rever and I ate dinner near the hospital."

"Hm."

He took a few steps in my direction and I retreated. "What's that supposed to mean?"

"You said you'd be back for dinner."

He ran his hands through his hair. "I know. Something came up. Didn't you get my voicemail?"

"No." I rubbed a hand over my face. "I had to turn off my phone an hour ago."

Ryker set his sunglasses on the dresser and began unbuttoning his shirt. "Why's that?"

"Because my parents won't stop calling. They're freaking out."

"Ah," he murmured, emptying his pockets. "I don't doubt it. Did you tell them where you were?"

"No," I snapped.

"Good."

I scrunched up my nose. "What's that supposed to mean?"

"We're leaving the day after tomorrow. I already

223

booked our flight. Send them a text. Tell them you took a road trip to clear your head, and you'll be home in a couple of days. There's no need to make them worry." He unbuckled his pants and pushed them down his legs. His belt buckle clanged against the tile floor.

My breathing accelerated, and I blinked, trying to erase the lust building inside of me with every piece of clothing he shed.

"I guess not," I whispered, staring at the wall above his head.

He settled onto the edge of the bed, wearing nothing but a pair of black boxer briefs. "Come here, Hattie," he said, his voice thick like honey.

"No." I shook my head.

He grinned. "I want to touch you. I missed you."

My eyes connected with his. "You did?"

"Always." He held out his hand. "I can't wait to go home. I hate it here. I've always hated it here."

"So do I." We gravitated to each other like two lodestones unable to resist the pull any longer.

He hauled me onto his lap and slid his arms around my waist. "We're never coming back."

"We're not?" I ran my hands up and down his arms. When he held me, I felt strong. Safe. Cherished.

"No." He brushed a gentle kiss across my lips, lingering there without moving, savoring the connection. The smoky flavor of bourbon coated his lips.

"Why not?" I whispered against his lips.

He unknotted my robe and pushed it down my shoulders. "We shouldn't have come here." His fingertips trailed over the swells of my breasts. Shivers danced down my spine, and I arched into his touch. Needing it. Craving it. Treasuring the urgency of his touch. "After tomorrow, I'm done with Ignacio and Rever. They'll be out of our lives forever."

"Why tomorrow? Why not today?"

"I have one more thing to do tomorrow and that's it." He flipped me onto my back and pressed his body into mine. His spicy scent clouded my thoughts and ignited a fever in my blood.

"You're going back to the hospital?"

He shook his head. "No. Rever and I need to take care of some loose ends at the Vargas compound. I'll be back late tomorrow night, and we'll be on the first flight out of here."

I traced the line of his jaw with my fingers. "Do you want me to come with you tomorrow?"

"No. Stay. You'll be safer here." His hands roamed my skin, exploring, caressing, memorizing every curve, and investigating every freckle.

"I was so bored today. I didn't leave the room. I stared at my computer screen all day."

"You didn't go to the pool or the beach?" His lips moved down my neck, splintering my thoughts.

I rolled my head to the side. "Tomorrow I'm going to go running," I mumbled, more as a promise to myself than him.

He paused and his eyes locked on mine. "Don't run too far. Stay close to the hotel."

Fear jolted through my body. "Why?"

He smiled as he cradled my stomach. "Do you have to question everything?"

"I don't like to be left in the dark." He kissed my belly, and I ran my fingers through his inky hair. "What are you doing?"

"Giving our baby a kiss. I think he missed me."

I placed my hand over his. "You're okay with this? I mean…" Words escaped me. There were so many reasons why I shouldn't have this baby and only one I should—I loved him, and by extension, the baby.

He smiled. "The timing isn't perfect. We don't have everything figured out. Senator Deveron isn't going to leave us alone, not yet anyway. But yes, I want you, and I want our baby."

Silent tears slid down my face. I was so fucking emotional. I wanted to slap myself sometimes. "Okay."

"Hey." He braced his body on his forearms, and a lock of hair brushed his forehead. "Don't cry. Everything is going to be okay."

I wiped my face. "I want that to be true, but sometimes I don't think we'll ever find a way out of this mess."

"We will."

"Maybe you're right. I'm just afraid the only way for us to be together is to give up everyone in our life. Our family. Our friends."

He held my gaze. "Yes," he said quietly, but he didn't seem upset by the prospect. He stroked my lower lip, and my heart flew like a bird inside of my chest.

"And you're okay with that?"

His eyes fell to my mouth. "Definitely. Are you?"

"I don't know."

He cupped my breasts as his thumb toyed with my nipples. "We have our own family now. If your family and friends don't want to be part of your life, it's their loss, but I think they'll come around."

I sucked in a sharp breath as his mouth trailed along my collarbone, and one of his hands slipped between my thighs. Stroke-by-stroke, touch-by-touch, kiss-by-kiss, my concerns dimmed until they faded away entirely.

"What are you doing to me?" I mumbled, my body humming with desire.

He rocked against me, and I circled my legs around his waist. "I'm showing you that we don't need anyone else as long as we have each other," he said with a lopsided grin.

I pushed his boxer briefs down his legs. "I like the sound of that."

He didn't waste a second before he pushed inside of me. A primitive sound vibrated deep in his throat. He twisted his hands in my hair as he captured my lips with bruising kisses that stole my heart and unshackled my soul. His hips hammered against mine in a brutal rhythm. I answered every thrust with one of my own. Clutching the sides of his face in my hands, I pulled his ear next to my mouth, and I whispered how much I loved him and that having him was enough. More than enough. Minutes later, we both cried out, climaxing in unison. It was the perfect beginning to our new life together. Just Ryker and me against the world. Always.

Chapter Twenty-Six

Ryker

"How much longer?" I asked, drumming my hands against the leather steering wheel.

"Any minute," Rever answered without glancing at me.

"Dammit, Rever. Text her. The mass is going to end in less than twenty minutes, and then we'll be fucked. I'm not getting into a gunfight on the church steps. I'm not religious, but I have limits."

He rolled down the window of the car and a wave of humid heat collided with the air-conditioned interior. "I did text her."

"Text her again."

"She knows we're here. She'll be here any second."

"Unless she set us up and we're about to get slaughtered."

His head whipped around. "She wouldn't do that."

"How do you know?"

"I just do."

"Fine, but if she doesn't walk out that door in the next ten minutes, I'm leaving. You can come with me, or you can stay. I don't care."

"She'll come," he murmured. "I'm not worried."

Time ticked by, second-by-second. I stared at the dashboard, willing ten minutes to pass. Part of me wanted Anna to keep her ass firmly planted on that wooden pew and reject Rever forever. The other part of me prayed she'd hurry the fuck up so I could put the final punctuation mark on this chapter of my life and move forward with Hattie and our baby.

With two minutes to spare, a petite woman with long black hair and a white full-length dress ran down the front steps, a straw tote bag clutched in her hand. She had a flawless olive complexion except the J-shaped scar near her right temple.

Rever flung the car door open. "Anna."

She waved her hands above her head. "Go back to the car. We can't do this today. They know something is going on."

"No," Rever yelled as he stalked up the steps. "You're coming with me today."

Anna glanced over her shoulder. A man dressed in jeans and a black t-shirt pushed open the front door of the church. "Go. Go without me," Anna yelled, moving slowly back up the steps.

Rever charged forward, grabbing her around the waist and tossed her over his shoulder. She pounded her fists on his back and kicked her legs. "*Suéltame. Suéltame, abusón*," she screamed, pleading for him to let her go.

"No."

"Dammit," I muttered.

I knew this wouldn't work. It was too simple. Too many things could go wrong. I snagged my gun off the center console and jumped out of the car. I held the gun in front of me and used the hood to shield my body. The man in the black t-shirt lifted a gun and aimed it at Rever's head. I didn't stop to think. I pulled the trigger.

The shot exploded through the air, drowning out the hum of the church hymn. His gun fell out of his hand, clattering down the steps and rolling to a stop in the street. He collapsed to his knees, clutching his bicep. His face drained of color as blood poured down his arm, splattering on the pristine ivory steps.

Screams drifted from inside the church walls. Rever set Anna on her feet. He stared at the scene, frozen in the moment, not moving, not breathing. Tears poured down her face as she stuffed her fist into her mouth and bent at her waist.

"Move." I pounded my hand against the hood. "Get in the car. We have to leave now."

Car tires squealed around the corner, and I dove in the front seat. Rever grabbed Anna's wrist and yanked her down the steps. She slapped his chest and clawed at his hand as she tried to break free. "He's my brother. I can't leave him. He's bleeding. Oh my God. This my fault. This was a dumb idea. I knew it."

Rever shoved her in the backseat and jumped in beside her. He looped his arms around her waist and rocked her back and forth. "It's going to be okay. It's just a flesh wound. Nothing more," he whispered next to her ear.

A car swerved around us, coming to an abrupt

stop perpendicular to the front bumper of our car, stopping the flow of traffic. I cranked the wheel to the right and slammed on the gas pedal. Our car jumped the curb, and my head whipped to the side. Sparks flew as the metal car rims grinded against the church steps. The minute we passed the car blocking the street, I jerked the steering wheel to the right, and we were back on the asphalt again.

Pop.

Pop. Pop. Pop!

Gunshots shattered the back window. Little slivers of glass showered over Rever and Anna's heads like rice at a wedding recessional.

"Drive faster," Rever barked, sheltering Anna's body with his.

I wove through the steady stream of cars, scooters, and golf carts clogging the main road circling the tiny island. "I'm going as fast as I can," I said through clenched teeth. "Take this and aim for their tires. Don't kill anyone," I yelled, tossing my gun over my shoulder. "We need to get them off our tail if we want to get into that helicopter and off this island in one piece."

Rever shoved Anna to the floorboard of the car and fired shot after shot out the back window until the road behind us cleared. I turned the corner and slammed on the brakes. Emilio's helicopter was waiting at the designated meeting spot. The roar of the blades drowned out the sounds of the ocean crashing against the slick, black rocks.

"Hurry. They will be here any second," I yelled as I flung open the door and ran to the helicopter, not waiting for Rever and Anna. He could take care of her. I'd done all I could for them.

As soon as we made it back to the Vargas compound, I was done with all of this shit, forever. I had supported my brother. I dropped everything to be at Ignacio's bedside, and he shoved it back in my face. I'd walked the line between two worlds and two lives for too many years to count. I couldn't do it anymore. I had a kid on the way, and if Ignacio or Rever wanted anything else from me, then tough shit. I'd given enough. Sacrificed enough.

My hands shook as I buckled my seatbelt. My eyes strained for any sign of Anna's security detail. Rever ducked his head and jogged to the door with Anna in his arms.

The minute Rever closed the door behind him, the helicopter lifted from the ground, and I took my first real breath since walking out of the hotel room this morning.

Still sobbing, Anna buried her head in Rever's lap. Rever stared out the window, his hand noticeably shaking as he stroked her hair.

"We did it," Rever said, his voice raspy.

"We did, but the next part is going to be the hardest," I replied, my eyes still trained on the shrinking island.

"What do you mean?"

"We have to wait for Juan Alvarez to retaliate."

"Do you think he'll do something?"

I snorted. "Yes."

"Well, that's Ignacio's problem. Anna and I will be gone tomorrow and so will you and Hattie. Ignacio can deal with it. Violence and revenge are his specialty."

"I hope you're right."

Chapter Twenty-Seven

Hattie

Ryker didn't come back to the hotel last night. He texted me late in the afternoon saying he wouldn't be back until sometime this morning. He and Rever went to visit Ignacio. Ryker told me he didn't want me to go with him, which was fine. I never wanted to step foot inside the Vargas compound again, much less see Ignacio. Ryker said he wasn't doing well, but that didn't soften my opinion of him.

As I exited the hotel, I turned on my iPod. I needed to run. I needed fresh air. We'd been in Mexico for almost four days, and I hadn't done much of anything except work on a research paper for my graduate degree. My back ached from being hunched over my laptop. Ryker warned me not to stray too far from the hotel grounds, but I hadn't jogged in days. I didn't plan to be gone long. Maybe thirty or forty minutes, and we were in the middle of Playa del Carmen, a tourist destination, not a cartel stronghold.

I rounded the corner, increasing my speed. At six thirty in the morning, the streets were empty except for a few people standing at the bus stop. I liked exploring the town this way. I could see traces of the sleepy fishing village before the tourist industry crept southward from Cancun.

With each stride, my feet pounded against the uneven sun-bleached pavement. Music screamed from my earbuds, blocking out the world. The faint tinge of ocean air tickled my nose. Sweat beaded at my temples. The humid air stuck in my lungs. Even this early in the morning, my clothes clung to my body like a second skin. I'd never get used to this weather.

I vaulted on and off the narrow sidewalk, avoiding signs, trashcans, and planters. My legs burned, but I pushed harder, hammering away at the cobwebs in my brain from too many sleepless nights and too much anxiety.

My phone repeatedly vibrated against my leg in the zipped pocket of my running shorts. Ryker was probably trying to reach me. He could wait. I'd decided to fly home today or tomorrow, regardless of whether his plans had changed. I wanted to go home. I hadn't seen Ryker much during the entire trip. He didn't need me here. I didn't belong here. As much as he denied it, this was his world.

I paused at the intersection as a white sedan turned the corner and came to an abrupt halt. A convoy of three trucks whipped around the corner, slamming on their brakes, effectively boxing me in.

A chill ghosted down my spine, and my skin prickled beneath the sheen of sweat. My heart squeezed painfully. I ripped my earbuds from my ears and draped the wire around the back of my neck. Panicked, I glanced over my shoulder for an escape route that didn't include walking by the cars. Just then, the passenger car doors opened. Men dressed in black exited the cars with assault weapons slung over their shoulders.

A scream bubbled up in my chest, but when I opened my mouth it resembled a whimper. Frozen with fear, I bit down on the inside of my cheek until the metallic taste of blood coated my mouth. My stomach flipped like an over-easy egg. Hundreds of thoughts raced through my mind, colliding like bumper cars as they vied for my attention.

I willed my legs to move, but dread cemented them to the ground.

"Rapido. Rapido," one man bellowed, waving his gun back and forth like a macabre music conductor.

Fuck. They were here for me. Blood drained from my face, and I swayed. Trembling, my iPod slipped from my boneless fingertips, cartwheeling down the sidewalk into the street. Strangely detached from reality, I watched it tumble around and around until it skidded to a stop.

Then, something clicked in my brain, and I ran. I ran like my life depended on it, and it probably did.

"Help me. Somebody help me," I screamed, not even pausing to glance over my shoulder. I vaulted over a collapsible sidewalk sign advertising breakfast. The toe of my sneaker caught the wooden edge, and it tipped over, sliding across the pavement.

"Agarrarla," a man yelled.

Strands of hair whipped around my face. Cold sweat poured down my back. My lungs burned. Blood thundered in my ears like a steam train, getting louder and louder with every stride.

Please don't let them catch me.

Please don't let them catch me.

Please don't—

Before I could finish the thought a third time, arms snaked around my waist, gouging the flesh of my stomach, centimeter by centimeter. The rubber soles of my sneakers scraped across the pavement. I lurched forward, battling him with every muscle fiber in my body, but instead of breaking his hold, we tumbled forward onto the sidewalk. Pain zigzagged up my arms as my hands crashed against the ground. Dirt and gravel dug into my flesh like shrapnel.

I scrambled forward, my fingernails clawing at the hairline fractures in the pavement as though I could rip them open and find refuge from the nightmare unfolding with lightning speed. Rust-colored blood from my hands streaked the pavement in parallel lines. He yanked my head backward by my hair, and my scalp pulsed with mind-splitting pain. Like a bull taunted by a matador in a bullfight, a red haze of bloodlust tinted my vision. I donkey-kicked backward over and over, relishing every grunt and groan spilling from the man's mouth.

I wouldn't win. I knew it. He knew it. He weighed at least a hundred pounds more than me. He had a gun. He had five men helping him, but I'd fight until I couldn't fight any longer. For me. For our baby.

"*Pinche puta,*" the man cursed next to my ear. Saliva splattered across the side of my face. Like a noxious gas, the smell of garlic and stale cigarette smoke infiltrated my lungs. I gagged, barely choking back the bile blistering the walls of my throat.

He shoved my face into the ground. My teeth rattled. Tears streamed unchecked down my sweat-stained face. Dirt coated my lips, crunching between my teeth.

"Fuck you. You piece of shit." I growled as I reached back and yanked a handful of his greasy hair, tearing it from the roots. My hand fell to the ground. Looking down, my stomach lurched when I saw a fistful of black hair threaded between my fingers.

"Did your boyfriend think we'd ignore his insult? That we wouldn't retaliate?" His hand coiled around the front of my neck, constricting the air to my lungs, and pressing with alarming accuracy against my jugular. I gasped for air. My body ached. Terror screamed through my veins.

My fingernails burrowed into his hand, scratching and mauling him like a feral alley cat. "I don't know what you're talking about," I said, but the words sounded more like hoarse whimpers.

"Shut the fuck up. All he had to do was mind his own business and stay the hell out of Mexico and away from Anna."

"No. No. No," I mumbled. My vision blurred from a combination of tears and lack of air.

Everything looked wavy and distorted. I drew my body into a tight ball. Ryker was supposed to protect me. He said he'd keep me safe, but he was nowhere to be found as his enemies stole my future, like cherry blossoms swept away in a spring wind. I had no one. Nothing.

Not again. Not again. I chanted, wishing my thoughts alone could stop this from happening. The butt of his gun collided with the side of my head, sandwiching my skull against the ground. Pain exploded inside my head, and white stars splashed behind my eyes. My vision tunneled to a pinprick, and then everything went dark.

Chapter Twenty-Eight

Ryker

I opened the door to our hotel room.

"Hattie?"

No answer.

Her suitcase sat on the luggage rack half packed. What the hell? Did she plan to leave without telling me? The soles of my shoes echoed against the creamy white tile floors as I crossed the room. I peeked inside the bathroom. Empty except for the faint hint of her crisp perfume.

Where the hell was she? I called her cell phone at least twenty times in the last five hours. She hadn't answered the phone in our hotel room either. I checked the pool and the beach. Nothing.

I settled into the chair across from the bed and rested my ankle on the opposite knee. Too exhausted to deal with the implications of her pending departure, I closed my eyes, concentrating on putting the last few days behind me.

Ignacio.

Rever.

Anna.

The Vargas Cartel.

For some reason, I had convinced Hattie to accompany me on this trip. Bringing her here didn't make sense, but when it came to Hattie, I was a greedy bastard. I refused to leave her at home and give her an opportunity to change her mind about me…about us. I didn't want her to create a new life without me because I couldn't and wouldn't live without her. Somehow she became my home. My everything.

My phone rang. I slipped it out of my pocket and checked the screen.

Thank God. It was Hattie.

"Hattie, where are you?"

"Ryker?" she said, her voice quivering.

I stood up. "Are you okay?"

"No," she whispered.

"Hand me the phone," a man yelled and my heart lurched.

"Hattie. Hattie. Talk to me. Who is that?"

"Is this Ryker Vargas?" A man's voice echoed through the phone.

"Yes. Who the fuck is this?"

"This is Juan Alvarez."

My stomach dropped, and the air whooshed out of my lungs. "What do you want?"

"What do you think I want? You invaded my turf and stole my daughter."

"She came willingly. She wanted to go with us."

"I don't give a fuck what she wanted, you mother fucker. You insulted my intelligence. You shot my son. You have seventy-two hours to return my daughter or—"

"That's not fucking happening. They're not even in Mexico anymore," I interrupted. Rever and Anna had booked a flight to Panama that departed hours ago.

"I know."

"Then you realize I can't return your daughter."

"Make it happen you piece of shit, or I'll have room service deliver Hattie's fingernails to your hotel room on a fucking silver platter, but I won't stop there. For every day that passes without Anna being returned to my home, I'll cut off another body part." He chuckled, a cold, lifeless sound that made the hair on my arms lift in protest. "Don't worry, I'll start with the small body parts. Ears. Fingers. Toes. Maybe a nose or an eye. And if she passes out, I'll pour rubbing alcohol on her face to make sure she doesn't miss a second of pain."

Rage boiled in my gut. For the first time in my life, I felt completely out of control. Revenge coiled around my chest like a Mexican black kingsnake. "No. You listen to me. If you touch a single hair on her head, I'll kill you and every one of your family members, and I won't do it with a single gunshot to the head. I'll carve them up into little pieces and watch them choke on their disgusting Alvarez blood. And when I'm done, I'll scatter their decayed body parts all over Mexico. Then, I'll come back for you, and cut out your intestines and feed them to you with a spoon while you bleed to death."

"Fuck you. Not if I kill you and your family first."

Before I responded, the phone went dead.

Admirable words, and not the first time I'd heard them either. Ten years had passed since someone uttered them to my face, which was the last time Ignacio managed to rope me into Vargas Cartel business.

Somehow the universe had boxed me into a corner, and I didn't have a choice. I called Ignacio. In order to get Hattie back, I'd need an army, and Ignacio was the only person who could give me that.

"Ignacio, it's Ryker," I said when he answered the phone. "I need your help. Juan Alvarez abducted Hattie." The words tasted like ash as they tumbled from my mouth.

"I'll help you on one condition." I clenched my phone, already knowing what he wanted. It was what he'd wanted for the last five years. "You have to take your place in the cartel. I mean it. From this point forward, you're all in, regardless of what happens."

Acid burned in my stomach. I never wanted it. I did everything to avoid it, but time was up. I'd run out of options. I sucked in a deep breath. My vision cleared, and my anxiety fizzled. There was something cathartic about accepting my fate. "You have a deal," I said.

My voice sounded cold and detached. Accepting his offer had stripped me of my humanity. With those four words, I had sacrificed my life and my future. For Hattie. For my child. I wished I could change it, but I'd never regret it. They were worth it. I owed it to her. I loved her, and I'd do anything to keep them safe, even if it meant giving her up and never knowing my child.

An eye for an eye.

Her life for mine.

My soul for hers.

A perfect trade.

I was grateful she ever wanted me, but I knew her love would evaporate the minute she discovered my fate. Until my death, I'd carry the bloody mantle of the Vargas Cartel on my shoulders.

It had happened so fast—too fast—like a tornado sweeping through my life and wrecking everything in its path. In a matter of days, I had lost everything. Everyone. Just like that, darkness rolled through me, filling my cells, coating my skin, corrupting my mind, and extinguishing the last flicker of light inside my soul.

It was done. Everything had come full circle, except this time there wouldn't be a happily ever after for Hattie and me.

Acknowledgements

Thank you for purchasing my book. I can't even begin to put to words what it means to me to be able pursue my love of writing.

To my husband, who puts up with a lot of craziness from me so I can get these stories out of my head.

To Limitless Publishing for continuing to support me, and Rachel Whitwam for squeezing me into her editing schedule.

Finally to Hype PR, all the bloggers, readers, and reviewers: I couldn't do this without you!

About the Author

After spending years practicing law and a million other things, Lisa decided to pursue her dream of becoming a writer and she must confess that inventing characters is so much more fun than writing contracts and legal briefs. A native of Colorado, she lives with her husband and three children in Denver.

Facebook:
https://www.facebook.com/lcardiff11

Twitter:
https://twitter.com/lcardiff_author

Website:
http://lisacardiff.com/

Goodreads:
https://www.goodreads.com/author/show/7692079.
Lisa_Cardiff

www.ingramcontent.com/pod-product-compliance
Lightning Source LLC
Chambersburg PA
CBHW030620120726
47904CB00006B/1973